IN THE SHADOW

SIR PATRICK BIJOU

PRELUDE

A handsome stranger in the dark crevices of her memories and dreams. A confused teenager who wants to run away from a tragedy. And a life about to be turned upside down.

"In the shadow" is a suspenseful coming-of-age dark fantasy novel filled with stomach-churning twists and turns.

Despite being identical twins, Arabella and Maisie couldn't be any more different.

Maisie has been extroverted, popular, and in love since middle school. Arabella is shy and, while she loves her sister, can't help but feel a little jealous that Maisie was lucky enough to find the love of her life so young.

As Arabella pines for an equally great love, her head is riddled with hazy memories and dreams about a mysterious man in the shadows.

Who is he? What does he want from her? How does she even know him?

As Arabella ponders these questions, she slowly realizes that the answers are slowly uncovering themselves.

What this mystery man shall bring into her life, she does not know. But she has a feeling he's going to change her... forever.

ABOUT THE AUTHOR

Sir Patrick Bijou lives and writes from the United Kingdom and is the author of several books on finance and fiction. He is known for his extraordinary skills in settling and negotiating peace settlements and international law and is a prodigious legal and political adviser. His diverse writing ability has been influenced by many experiences, making him the success he is today.

Sir Patrick has written many books and articles about the liberation of people, highlighting the issues of those whom the literary world of creative writing has not enlightened. His expedition into content writing has made him a remarkably inspired author and professional communicator.

He has written over 32 non-fictional and fictional books spanning different genres.

Finding his Books.

To find out more about Sir Patrick, visit his website.

www.sirpatrickbijou.com
www.bijouebook.com

The sunlight gently touched Arabella's face. She slowly opened her eyes. She looked around the bedroom she was in, she didn't recognize it before. Arabella sat up in bed and looked around to gain familiarity with the bedroom. It was as if she opened her eyes in the 1700s. There were drapes over the bed; there was a brown antique wardrobe that was against the wall-some of the drawers were opened. Arabella knew she was in a dream. She had to be. There was no way it could be real, could it?

"Glad to see you're awake." A voice said coming from the window.

Arabella saw that a figure was by the window covered by the curtains. She stood up and slowly walked to the figure.

"Don't come any closer." The figure said.

"What? Why?" she asked. "Who are you? Where am I?" "In due time, we will meet." The figure said.

"Is this real?" Arabella looked around the room, trying to see if she would notice something. "I mean-are you even real?"

"I am." The figure whispered in her ear.

A cold chill went down her spine. Arabella couldn't move. Although she was scared, she was somewhat at ease. Her mind was confused.

"How will I know it is you?" Arabella softly asked. "When the sun and moon align." The figure answered. "I'll be watching you."

As Arabella stood there with a confused look on her face, she was trying to piece everything together. "Arabella?" the figure said. "It's time to wake up." Arabella opened her eyes. She was sitting in the backseat of the car with her twin sister. She looked over; Maisie was on her phone with her boyfriend. Arabella then looked at her mom, who was reading a book she had brought on the trip. Her mom had brought enough books with her on the trip to open up a library. Arabella grabbed her notebook and began writing her dream down.

She was curious to know who she was talking to in her dream. What scared her the most was not him knowing her; it was her not being terrified of him.

"We have successfully made it back home." Arabella's dad said loud enough for the three of them to hear.

Finally," Maisie said. "I'm ready to see my friends.

"I'm thinking next summer we should go to the beach." Her dad said.

"Dad, can we get through the year first?" Arabella asked.

"Bella is right," Maisie said, locking her phone. "We are both going to college next year."

"Both of our girls are going to the same college." their mother said. "I'm going to miss these family trips to the cabin."

"Oh, mom," Maisie said, throwing her head back on the seat.

Arabella looked over at Maisie. They both begin to laugh. Maisie and Arabella were similar in many ways. They were both intelligent, and both got accepted to the best school in Toronto. Despite their similarities, Maisie and Arabella were different. Maisie was outgoing and pushy; she fantasized about life. Plus, she was the captain of the cheerleading team in high school. She received the homecoming crown when she was just a freshman in high school. Arabella, on the other hand, was the opposite. She was shy and timid. She was optimistic. Not just about school but everything else. Despite the girls being different, they were both extremely close. The girls practically did everything with each other. Arabella couldn't see her life without her sister.

Tom drove into their driveway and put the car in park. The four of them all got out, grabbed their bags, and walked to the front door. Arabella was happy to be home but nervous at the same time. It was an adjustment to being back.

Arabella opened the door to her bedroom, dropped her duffel bag by the door, and walked around the room. There were picture frames on the dresser, nightstand, and desk forcing her not to glance. Arabella sat on the bed and looked at her phone. She had missed calls and messages from her best friends. As she was writing a text back to them, Maisie knocked on the door.

"Hey, Mai," Arabella said. "What's up?"

"Want to go to Emilio's?" Maisie asked.

"Um." Arabella didn't want to go, but she couldn't think of a reason not to go. "Yeah. Let's go."

Great," Maisie said, smiling.

Twenty minutes later, Maisie and Arabella were at the bar. The best bar in town where the high school students come and relax with tourists looking for a nice dinner with good service.

Maisie opened the door to the bar, and they both walked in. Arabella could see the same customers coming to the bar for years, sitting down, eating, and laughing. As they walked through the crowd of tables, Arabella could see everyone staring at her. She questioned herself being in the bar while they walked past the pool tables where the high school students played.

"Hey, there is Noah," Maisie said. "Are you going to be alright?"

"Yeah, go ahead." Arabella lied. She watched as Maisie walked over to Noah, who was the captain of the hockey team. They were a 'high school it' couple. They have been dating since middle school. From every holiday to every birthday, Maisie and Noah were always seen together. Noah waved at Arabella; she waved back. Arabella found herself at the bar with a glass of water in front of her. Now and then, she would glance at Maisie and Noah. Arabella wanted what her sister had. She wanted long kisses, midnight walks, and picnic dates. Most importantly, she wanted to be seen. Arabella took a sip of her water.

"Hey." a soft voice said behind her.

Arabella looked up and saw her two friends sitting down next to her.

"When did you get back in town?" Her friend, Scott, asked. He took the bowl of peanuts and started eating them.

"An hour ago," Arabella answered.

"We see Maisie couldn't wait to get to Noah." Her other friend, Eva, said. "Those lovebirds need to get married already."

"Did you tell your parents about Boston?" Scott asked. "I haven't," Arabella replied. Arabella forgot to mention to her parents that she got accepted to the university in Boston with everything that has happened. She didn't know how she was going to tell them. Her parents were trying to keep her close to town after what had happened.

"You got some nerve showing your face here after what you did." someone said behind her.

Arabella turned around. She saw a tall man with blondish hair standing there. He was wearing a blue jean jacket and dark jeans. He was holding a beer bottle in his hand. Arabella could tell he was drunk. It wasn't the first time the man talked to her while he was drunk. "Peter," Arabella said. She stood up.

"I thought I made myself clear for you not to show up until after the funeral," he told her. "You think you Holloways are above us, so entitled," he added.

"I have apologized over and over again to you and your family," Arabella said. "What can I do?"

"Can you bring my sister back?" he asked.

"I'm sorry, Peter," Arabella said. "I wish I could bring her back. I wish it were me instead. Every day." she added.

Arabella watched him finish his beer and then bang it on the table.

"You killed my sister Bella," he exclaimed. He started walking towards her.

As Peter walked towards Arabella, a tall guy stepped in front of him. He had brown hair that was long enough for him to run his fingers through. Arabella watched as he spoke to Peter, and then Peter placed the broken bottle down and walked away. The guy turned around to look at Arabella. His eyes were golden brown, and his skin was fair. She looked at him up and down, getting a full glance at him. He was wearing a white-collar shirt that showed off his broad shoulders and muscles and black jeans. She noticed that he had a tattoo on his forearm. Arabella had never seen him around town before.

"Are you alright?" he asked her. He walked closer to her, so it was just them two.

"Yes, I am fine," she answered. "And so is everyone else," she said, looking around the bar.

"Bella, are you okay?" Maisie asked, coming to her side with Noah.

"I'm fine, Mai," Arabella answered. "He came to my rescue."

The three all looked at him.

"Thank you so much." Maisie thanked him. "I think that's enough excitement for one night."

"Come on. I'll take you home." Noah said. "Thank you, man, again."

"Yeah, come on, Bella," Scott said.

"Thank you," Arabella said, looking at the guy. She smiled at him and then turned to walk away with Eva and Scott.

Arabella and Maisie were sitting in the kitchen with Noah, Eva, and Scott. They had sat in silence for a while until Scott spoke.

"That was intense," Scott said.

"I thought Peter left for Seattle," Maisie said.

"He never left," Noah told her. "Said he needed to be here with his mom."

"I think it's safe to say that we all need a good night's rest," Eva told all of them.

Yeah." Arabella agreed. She couldn't help but think who the guy was from the bar.

Arabella said goodbye to Eva and Scott while Maisie was saying goodbye to Noah.

"Okay, we will be here tomorrow to pick you up," Scott told Arabella.

"Sounds good." She spoke.

"Alright. We'll see you tomorrow." Eva hugged her.

"I'll see you tomorrow as well," Noah said to Maisie. He kissed her on the forehead. "I'm glad you are alright, Bella."

"It was good to see you, Noah." Arabella smiled.

"I'll see you tomorrow," Maisie said, walking Noah to the door.

Maisie turned to Arabella and sighed. Maisie could sense that Arabella was defeated. She walked towards her sister and hugged her.

"It'll be alright," Maisie said. "One day at a time."

Later that night, Arabella couldn't sleep. She lay awake in her bed, staring at the ceiling. She couldn't help but think about her dream and the guy from the bar.

"When the sun and moon align."

Those words repeated over and over in her head. She grabbed her phone and searched for anything about the alignment that was supposed to happen.

After a few minutes of searching, she found something. The alignment of the sun and moon was scheduled to happen in three weeks. As she read the article further, she found that it only happens every ten years. There was going to be a gathering to see the alignment at Cove Creek. She placed her phone down on the nightstand and threw her back down on the pillow. Not only was there going to be an eclipse from someone she was supposed to meet from her dream, but it was going to be shown at the one place she hasn't been back to in months.

Arabella couldn't think, let alone relax. Before she knew it, she was sleeping.

BEGIN FLASHBACK.

"Hey, I can drive," Arabella said.

"Bella, you've been drinking," Tessa said.

"So what?" Arabella asked. "We've all been drinking." "Oh, come on," Scott said. "Let's go."

"Stop being a party pooper," Arabella said to Tessa. "Live a little."

"So, Tessa, what do you say?" Eva asked. "Are you going to come with us and have the greatest night of your life, or are you going to go home?"

The three of them stared at Tessa for an answer. Then she smiled, and Arabella jumped for joy.

"Let's ride," Scott said.

The four of them got into the car and started driving away from the house party. Arabella turned the volume knob up to the radio. As they were all singing and shouting with excitement, Arabella was too drunk to notice the stop signs. She ran a stop sign; she turned to look at her friends.

"Don't stop," Tessa shouted. She took the liquor bottle from Scott and drank some of it.

"Whoa!" Eva shouted.

As Arabella drove and ran through each stop sign, she didn't see the headlights on Tessa's face. The SUV t-boned Arabella's car. Arabella could hear voices coming from outside the car. Arabella looked around and saw that Eva and Scott were okay, but Tessa wasn't. "Tessa," Arabella shouted, trying to gain consciousness.

"Bell, she's not waking up," Scott said. "Look."

Tessa had a bloodstain on her shirt. Scott lifted her shirt, and they saw that her stomach was black and purple, and her stomach was sliced open.

"Oh, my God," Eva said.

As people from the town were helping the four of them out of the car while the ambulance was on its way. Arabella was wrapped in a blanket while Eva and Scott were on the curb, trying to regain consciousness. "Bella." her parents were yelling, pushing through the crowd of people.

Arabella starts crying as she runs towards them. Her parents hug her while kissing her head.

"Are you okay?" her dad asked.

I think so," she answered.

"Mr. Holloway?" Fred, one of the detectives at the station, said.

"Yeah, Fred?" Arabella's dad said, turning around. He wiped his face. "What is it?"

"Tessa Mavericks didn't make it out of the accident," Fred said.

"No," Arabella screamed. She looked at her mother, who was trying to comfort her. Arabella moved away, screaming and shouting. "This is all my fault."

"Bella, don't say that." her father said.

Arabella looked at her parents with tears rolling down her face. When her parents walked closer to her, Arabella took the blanket off and ran from them. "Bella." She heard her dad yell.

Arabella didn't look back. She couldn't believe it; her friend was gone. And it was Arabella's fault. She didn't know where or to what she was running towards but she didn't stop. She felt her head pounding, and as she tried to shake the fact that it was just the accident that had made her body ache, she fell into a ditch. As she tumbled down the hill hitting the trees, she started to remember the days when she was younger. She and her twin sister are playing outside in the treehouse that their dad had built for them. She then landed head-first on a log and went unconscious.

Arabella was going in and out of consciousness. She felt her body being lifted from the ground and brought to someone's chest. She slowly opened her eyes; she saw a man. He had black hair, or at least she thought he did. "Who are you?" She asked.

"Shh," he said. "You're safe."

And that somehow made her feel safe. Before closing her eyes, she noticed that he had a scar on his neck. END FLASHBACK.

Arabella slowly opened her eyes. She looked at her phone; it was the first day back to school. Arabella lay in her bed for a few minutes until she finally got the courage to get out of bed. She pushed back the blanket and stood up, then walked to the bathroom. She stared at herself in the mirror. She was nervous about going to school. But she knew she couldn't hide anymore. "Hey, Bell," Maisie said.

"Oh, hey." Arabella quickly grabbed her toothbrush and the toothpaste.

"I'm going to school early with Noah," Maisie informed her. "Save me a seat at lunch?"

"Of course," Arabella answered.

"Okay, great," Maisie said. "I gotta go." She grabbed her hair tie and eyeliner. She kissed Arabella on the cheek and walked out of the bathroom.

Arabella went downstairs; she saw her parents in the kitchen, eating breakfast, and drinking their coffee. "Good morning," Arabella said to both of them. "Morning, sweetheart." Her mom said, smiling.

"Hey, that night of the accident," Arabella began to say, "the person that brought me back home."

"Yeah, what about him?" Her father asked.

"You know who it was?" Arabella asked. "I want to thank him," she added.

"I think it was one of the locals." Her mother responded.

"It was months ago. I'm sure the kid left town after that." Her father added.

After seventeen years of knowing when her parents were lying or telling her the truth, she knew they were lying.

"Well, I have to get to school." Arabella looked down at her phone. There was a message from Scott. "I'll see you guys after."

Tom and Lucia watched Arabella walk out of the house. They both looked at each other. They knew Arabella was going to find out eventually. All the years they have been protecting their daughters, were coming to an end. "We are going to have to tell them," Lucia told Tom.

"Yeah, I know." Tom agreed.

Scott drove into the school parking lot. The three of them got out of the car and started walking to the entrance.

"Hey Bella." one of the hockey players said. "Good to see you."

"Hey, Lance," Arabella said, smiling.

"Today is going to be a great day," Eva said.

"I thought we would sign up for one of the committees," Scott said as they all walked into the building.

"Sounds like a great idea," Eva said. "What do you think, Bell?"

"Maybe the decoration committee," Arabella suggested. She looked around the hallway. Everyone that walked past her was smiling and telling her that they were glad to see her.

As the three of them were discussing the committee, someone called out for Arabella. She saw that it was the principal.

"I have to go, but I'll see you in class." She told them. Eva and Scott both nodded.

"Yes, Mr. Wilson," Arabella said.

"I know this is your first day of school like everyone else, but I was wondering if you could show this gentleman around?" he asked.

"Of course." She answered.

"Thank you, Ms. Holloway." He said. "Mr. James?"

A tall guy with brown hair turned around. It was the same guy from the bar.

"You?" Arabella said.

"You two know each other?" Mr. Wilson asked.

"Not exactly." She answered.

"Well, this works out perfectly then." Mr. Wilson said. "Mr. Wilson, you have a phone call." The secretary said. "Well, if you both would excuse me." He said.

Arabella and the guy stood there in silence, staring at each other.

"We better get going." The guy finally said.

"Right." She agreed. She took his schedule, and they walked out of the office.

The two walked in silence until they got to a room in the school that was worth mentioning, and then both of them continued to walk in silence again.

"This is the library," Arabella said.

"I can see that." He said.

"Right." She said, biting her lip. "Listen, let's cut the small talk."

"I didn't know we were talking." He said.

"Humor me." She told him. "I want to say thank you for last night."

"You don't need to thank me," he told her. "I was just doing what anyone would have done," he added.

"Well, I'm glad you were there." She said. "If I may ask, where were you in the bar?"

"I was sitting by the jukebox." He answered.

Arabella soon realized that the jukebox was on the other side of the bar. Arabella couldn't imagine him running and leaping and no one seeing him.

"Bella?" Eva yelled. "We are going to be late for class." "Coming," Arabella shouted.

"English?" He asked.

"Yes." She responded.

"Mr. Antoine?" He asked.

"Yeah." Arabella gave him a surprised look.

"We better go. Don't want to be late for class," he told her.

They both walked into the classroom. Arabella found an empty seat next to Eva.

"Is that the guy from the bar?'' she asked her.

"Yep," Arabella answered.

"He's cute," Eva stated.

Arabella looked at Eva and watched Eva shrug her shoulders. Arabella watched the guy take a seat by the window. She wanted to know his name and him.

As class started, Julian couldn't help but keep his eyes on her. He was drawn to her, and he didn't know why.

He was determined to find out. Julian could smell her scent from miles away. He watched as she turned to talk to the blonde-haired girl that was sitting next to her. Her long black hair came down to the middle of her back, and there were no words to describe how beautiful her brown skin was. And every time he looked into her eyes, he was mesmerized.

Julian walked into the school's ice rink. He saw a bunch of the high school guys in the rink practicing in front of the coach.

"Hey, I didn't know you played hockey?" Noah asked. Julian turned his head, and he saw the guy that was at the bar. He was holding his hockey stick and wearing his gear.

"I tend to know a little bit of the sport," Julian said. He watched as the guys on the ice played a game of scrimmage".

"Show us what you got then." One of the guys said, walking out on the ice.

Julian loved a good game, especially one that involved seeing who was the best. Julian borrowed another player's gear and got on the ice. As the coach blew his whistle, Julian quickly smacked the puck across the ice to the other player on his team. He used his speed and his strength to glide past the guys and smack the puck past the goalkeeper.

The players played two games, which lasted roughly twenty minutes, and in each game, Julian scored a point. The coach blew his whistle for the game. As everyone cheered and teased each other, the guy from the bar skated to Julian.

"Good game." The guy said. "You are faster than the other dudes on the team, man." He added.

"Thanks." Julian took off his gloves.

"I'm Noah, by the way." The guy introduced himself. He held out his hand, waiting for Julian to shake his hand.

"Julian." Julian shook his hand.

"Mr. James, I never saw anything like what you just did on the rink. Have you ever played hockey before?" The coach asked. "I'm looking for someone to fill the position of forward if you're interested." He finished. Julian looked at Noah, who was egging him to take the position.

"I would love to coach." Julian accepted.

Later that day, Julian found himself sitting outside with everyone else. He was sitting two tables across from where she was sitting. Julian hasn't eaten in two days, but he didn't mind; he wanted to be there. Watching her. She had his attention. And he could sense that he had hers too.

"I was thinking we would set up for the fundraiser to raise money for the school trip that is happening next month." Julian heard the guy with dark brown hair say.

"I think that's perfect." The blonde hair girl said. "Maisie and Noah will be there as well." Julian heard the girl say. "It's always good to have the cheer team and hockey team at the fundraiser."

"Have you guys talked?" The dark-haired guy asked.

"I thanked him." The girl said. "I still don't know his name."

"Why don't you go over there and talk to him?" he asked her.

Julian looked at her as she was thinking about whether or not to walk to the table.

"Go." the blonde hair girl said.

"Okay." the girl said. She stood up from the picnic table and began to walk towards him. "Hey."

"Hey," Julian said to her.

"Mind if I sit?" She asked.

"Of course, please sit," he answered.

"I never caught your name." She said.

"Julian." He answered.

"I'm-"

"Bella." He interrupted her. "It's nice to meet you." He held out his hand, waiting for her to shake his."

"It's a pleasure to meet you." She placed her hand in his. She quickly pulled away when she felt that his hand was cold.

"Sorry," Julian said.

"So Julian, where are you from?" She asked, ignoring what she just felt. "You're not from around here."

"I'm from Louisiana." He answered. "My family moved here a month ago in search of a different view."

"You're a long way from Louisiana." She told him.

Julian chuckled.

As lunch ended, Julian and Bella were walking in the hallway, talking. Julian actually enjoyed hearing her talk about her life. He felt as if he knew her whole life. They both walked into the Biology class and sat down next to each other.

"I realized I have been talking. I haven't let you talk. I'm sorry." She apologized.

"I enjoy hearing you talk," Julian told her.

"Tell me about your family?" She asked. "What are they like?"

"My family is quite boring. Your typical boring family." He answered. "Besides, I don't think my family could ever top yours. Your dad is the mayor of the town." "And every day, I wish that my family was normal." She told him. "I think everyone has something they don't want anyone to know about their family. Whether it's the dad having a secret life or-" She looked at Julian. For a split second, both of them were lost in their own thoughts.

"I'm sorry." She said. "I said too much," she whispered to herself.

Julian wanted to know more about her. There was something she was keeping to herself, but also so was he. He knew that if he continued the friendship with Bella, it would come at a price. Julian wanted to know why he was drawn to her. Apart from him wanted her for himself, but the other wanted to keep her at a distance. Julian was walking home when Bella ran next to him. "Hey." She said. "Mind if I walk with you?"

"Not at all." He answered. He placed his hands in his pockets and continued to walk in silence.

"How was your first day?" She asked him.

"It was good." He quickly said.

"You're not much of a talker, are you?" She asked him.

"Why do you say that?" He asked. He glanced over at her.

"I was talking your ear off today, and you never stopped me." She explained. "You either have nothing to say, or you didn't want to be rude and tell me to shut up."

"As I said, Bella, I enjoy hearing you talk." He explained to her. "It's nice not to have to talk. A breath of fresh air."

"Poetic." She smiled. "Are you hungry?"

Julian could have said no, but instead, he told her that he was. He was, but due to his impeccable diet, he wouldn't sustain from eating human food. He was craving something more prominent.

"Good." She smiled. She led him to the bar.

They walked into the bar and sat down next to the window.

"This is on me to say thank you again for yesterday." She told him.

"Thank you, but I can't let you do that." He told her. Julian watched as Bella frowned. He was making it hard for her to be a decent human being.

"My father would kill me if he saw that you were paying," Julian said. He smiled at her and picked up the menu.

"What can I get you both?" Tilly, one of the waitresses, asked.

"Hey Tilly," Bella greeted, "can I get a deluxe burger with fries and a chocolate shake?"

And for you?" Tilly asked Julian.

"A chicken salad will be fine," Julian answered. "And water?"

"A deluxe burger with fries and chocolate shake. And a chicken salad with water." Tilley repeated the orders. "It'll be right out."

"Thank you, Tilly." Bella smiled. "Eating like that, I think you were making me look bad."

"I'm on a strict diet," he told her.

"The more we talk, the more you surprise me," she stated. "You're different from everyone else here in town."

"Is that a good thing?" he asked.

"I haven't decided yet." She responded.

As they both sat at the table, both of them staring into each other's eyes, Julian couldn't help but feel as if time was slowing down. It was as if they were the only ones in the bar. Everything was growing quiet around them. Julian found his focus. It was her. He found the missing piece to make him feel whole again. The combination of both affinity and chemical compatibility that they possessed was, in fact, what drew him to her. It was only a matter of time before she knew what he was.

Later that evening, Julian walked Bella home. He told her the truth when he said that he enjoyed hearing her talk. Her voice was calming, and it put his body at ease. He can admit that he has had his fair share of women, but there was something about Arabella that he couldn't resist. He knew that that was his weakness, but also, just maybe that could be his strength. Suddenly, there was rain coming down from the sky. Julian grabbed Bella's hand, and they began running to a nearby roof.

"Are you alright?" He asked her. He looked at her up and down to see if there was anything wrong with her.

"Yes, yes. I'm fine." She laughed. "Just a little rain." She looked up at him.

Their bodies were a hand distance apart. Julian could smell the sweet scent of strawberry shampoo from her hair. He could hear her heart racing with excitement. She wanted him to kiss her, and he knew it. He took a step back, took off his leather jacket, and placed it over her head.

"Let's get you home," Julian said, leading her out from under the roof.

Julian and Bella ran up the front porch steps shaking off the rain from their clothes.

"Thank you," Bella said. "Second time you came to my rescue. Any more of those, and people are going to start to think I can't take care of myself."

"Right." Julian smiled.

Bella took off the leather jacket and held it out for Julian.

"Keep it." He told her.

"Thank you, and thank you for dinner." She grinned. "Arabella." Julian heard an older soft voice yell from inside the house.

"I better go." She whispered. "See you at school." "Okay." Julian smiled back.

Julian watched her walk inside and shut the front door behind her. He quickly left and started heading home. His mind was filled with images of Arabella. From the way she talked to the way, she put her hair behind her ear when she is trying to concentrate. He knew he was going to enjoy his time in Toronto.

Julian opened the door to his house twenty minutes later. It was quiet, too quiet. He walked through the foyer and into the kitchen.

"Where were you?" a voice asked behind him.

"I went to eat dinner." Julian grabbed a blood bag from the fridge and turned around. He saw his mother standing there with a disappointed look on her face. She looked down at the blood bag and then let out a sigh.

"He was with that girl from school." His sister, Isla, said, coming through the back door.

"She's no one," Julian assured them.

"Oh, really?" Isla asked.

"I find that very hard to believe." His mother grumbled. "Julian, we have been over this. You can't hang out with the locals. We are here to find the person that killed all those people."

"Mother, please." Julian pleaded. "I am capable of keeping both of them apart."

"What is going on here?" His father asked, coming from behind Isla.

"Julian met someone." His mother answered.

"That's great." His father rejoiced. He walked past Isla and walked to the bar. He grabbed the bourbon and a glass.

"A human, Edmund." His mother added.

"Interesting." His father finished pouring the bourbon into the glass. He took a sip and then turned to Julian. "Julian, your mother is right. We are here doing a duty. We cannot afford to make roots here in this town." "Isla, have you seen images of this girl?" His mother asked. "Who is she?"

"I have, but she isn't familiar to me," Isla responded. "Need to find out who this girl is." His mother demanded.

Julian looked at the three of them and walked past them in disappointment. Julian opened the door to his bedroom; there were books sprawled on the floor of the room. His bed was made, probably because he never slept in it. In fact, Julian didn't do much sleeping. He walked to the balcony of his room and stared out into the darkness. He couldn't believe his family. A part of him was angry, but the others knew why they said it. He didn't come to Toronto to look for love or any friendship with the natives in town. They were there to track down the new bloodsucker that was killing off everyone that came in its path.

Julian closed his eyes. He could smell Bella's sweet scent. He inhaled, having the scent consume his lungs. Somehow it made him warm. He could hear the leaves rustling on the trees and ground. Julian never asked to become what he was. One day, he was fighting with the British army, and the next day, he was a human bloodsucker. He has been seventeen for the last hundred years, and the only family he knew were the three trying to help him focus. He couldn't blame them for that.

"Are you okay?" Isla asked.

"If you came here to gloat, you're wasting your time." He told her.

"No." She said. "I came to see if you were alright, brother." She corrected him.

Julian felt her presence next to him. Without looking at her, he felt her hand touch his.

"We are just trying to protect you, Julian." She said. "Trying to protect all of us."

"I know." He looked at her. "Isla, she is different."

"You imprinted on her, didn't you?" She asked.

Julian quickly looked away. Imprinting only worked with werewolves, but it could happen with vampires. The last vampire imprinted on a human was killed for putting the human in danger. The Council announced that humans and vampires could never coexist. The human was left with a clean memory and no reconciliation with her lover.

"What are you going to do?" Isla asked.

"I have to protect her," Julian responded.

"And if that protection meant you were dying?" She asked.

"I'm willing." He said, staring into the forest that was behind their house.

The next day, Arabella woke up feeling well-rested. She felt her mind was put at ease. She walked into the bathroom and started brushing her teeth.

"Hey," Maisie said, walking into the bathroom. "I didn't see you after school. Where'd you go?"

"I went to dinner at the bar," Arabella said, rinsing her mouth out. "With the guy that stopped Peter the other night."

"Really?" Maisie gave her a surprised look. "His name is Julian, right?"

"Yeah, how do you know?" Arabella asked.

"Noah told me that he tried out for the hockey team yesterday," Maisie explained. "Noah said he was excellent and that he got a position on the team," she added.

"Really?" Arabella placed her toothbrush in the holder and dried her hands on the hand towel.

Arabella was determined to get to know Julian, even if it meant she had to pry. Something about him told her that he was bad news, and she couldn't ignore the feeling anymore.

Arabella was in the hallway in front of her locker when Eva and Scott came by.

"So rumor has it that you were at the bar with Mystery Man," Eva stated. She leaned against the locker and gave Arabella a stern look.

"A rumor, huh?" Arabella scoffed. She placed her books into her locker and then closed them.

"Is it true?" Scott asked.

"So what if it is?" Arabella replied. "We just went for dinner. No harm in going to dinner."

"We just want you to be careful." Scott cautioned. "You barely know him."

"I'm well aware of that." Arabella snapped. She looked at both of them with a sad smile. "I know you both are worried about me. I'm here to tell you that I am fine. Julian and I are just friends. It's the last year of high school, and I don't think I can take on a relationship and Mr. Antoine's strict English class."

Eva and Scott both looked at each other and shrugged their shoulders. Arabella knew that they were just trying to protect her. After all, they were right; Arabella didn't know anything about Julian. But she intended to find out.

"Can we please get to class?" Arabella asked both of them.

"Yeah," Eva answered.

"I have to go but meet you guys at lunch," Scott said. Across town, Tom was sitting in his office looking at the police reports sent to his office regarding the missing persons in town. All the deaths were consistent: animal attacks. He placed the files on the desk, turned around, and looked out the window. He couldn't focus. His mind was racing. He wanted to give everyone in town an explanation for the animal attacks, but also he needed to talk to his daughters. Where would he even start? That seemed to be the question that had been lingering in his mind from the start of the day.

"Tom?" a soft voice said, coming into the office.

Tom turned around and saw his wife Lucia closing the door behind her.

"Lucia, what are you doing here?" He asked. "Is everything alright?"

"Tom." She said again. "We need to tell them the truth." She placed her hands in his. Tears were coming down from her eyes. He wiped them away.

"I know, but we can't." He said. "They wouldn't be able to forgive us."

"Arabella is asking questions." Lucia reminded him. "It's just a matter of time before Maisie starts asking. I thought you said it was going to work. Make them forget."

"Lucia, if we tell them we are putting their lives in danger." He noted.

"Not telling them, we are putting their lives in jeopardy." She corrected him. "We have to call her. She'll know what to do."

Tom pulled Lucia to him and gently rubbed his hand on her head. Lucia and Tom have been practically married since they were in grade school. When they finally did marry, Lucia's family wasn't there. They never did approve of Tom and what he did for a living. So the only witnesses to their wedding were Tom's mother and Lucia's childhood friend. Years passed, and they didn't give birth to a child until one day, Tom's mother took Lucia to see an older woman. Lucia vaguely remembers the day when she met the woman, but she does recall waking up the next day with a headache and terrible morning sickness. As Tom and Lucia both tried to put the pieces together as to how it happened, Lucia couldn't have been more thrilled. Lucia gave birth to two beautiful girls on Halloween. Both Tom and Lucia watched as their daughters grew up, and they both couldn't have been happier. They were finally a family. Time passed, and their daughters got older, but Tom and Lucia began noticing small changes in their daughters' lives. They both knew they had to protect their daughters.

One day, He came for her. He chose her. And He loved her. Tom and Lucia took their daughters and ran. They were running for years until He did come for her again. But now, Lucia and Tom were still parents, and they had to protect their daughters because that's what they had to do.

Arabella was sitting outside with Eva and Scott, with some of the other students from the committee discussing the fundraiser on Halloween, which was also Arabella and Maisie's birthday. As they debated ideas of a theme, Arabella sees Julian with Noah and some of the other hockey jocks. He must have known she was looking at him because he looked over at her. They stared at each other for what seemed like an eternity.

"Bell, do you think we should dress up for the fundraiser?" Eva asked.

"Yeah, we should," Arabella answered. "It's not Halloween if we don't dress up."

"Now I have to find a costume." One of the girls whined.

"And I have to make a costume." Another one groaned. "Can't you buy something from the store?" Scott asked, trying to settle their problems.

"Can you?" A girl mimicked. "Can't just buy any costume. It has to be the costume. We want every boy to stop and stare at us. We can't just wear anything." She explained.

"I'm glad I'm not a girl," Scott said jokingly.

Arabella looks over at Julian; he is gone. Arabella meant what she said to Eva and Scott about not being ready for a relationship. She had enough on her plate, and she couldn't fathom taking on a relationship. But also, she couldn't lie and say she wasn't attracted to him because she was. His charm and the mystery he carried were what she craved. But at what cost?

After school, Arabella and her friends were rummaging through the school's fundraiser decorations. Since they suggested a theme, Mrs. Davenport, the director of all the fundraiser committees, provided them with Halloween props. The three of them begin taking the boxes that they needed from the school's storage closet and setting them outside in the gym.

"Hey, we came to help," Maisie said, walking towards them with Noah.

"Great," Eva said. "If you both can start putting the boxes that are in the gym in Mrs. Davenport's office." she pointed to a pile of boxes by the bleachers.

"On it," Noah told her.

"How many more boxes?" Scott asked. "I think there is enough in here to have three Halloween fundraisers."

"Two more boxes should be fine," Arabella answered. "We want to make sure the fundraiser is perfect."

They begin to rummage through more boxes for ten minutes. Once the three of them realized there were enough decorations, Arabella closed the storage closet and began to walk out, following Eva and Scott.

As Arabella was walking out, she heard a noise coming from the girls' locker room. She wondered why anyone would be in the locker room after school hours.

"Be right back," Arabella shouted to Eva.

"Don't belong," Eva said.

Arabella walked into the girls' locker room. She noticed that all the showers were running-there was steam fogging the mirrors.

"Hello?" She said. "Anyone in here?"

The showers were probably running for a while, she thought to herself. She quickly turned them off and slowly walked around the locker room, trying to investigate. As she investigates, she hears a loud bang when Eva walks into the locker room. Arabella jumps in fear, and she then looks over at Eva.

"What are you doing?" She asked.

"Thought I heard something," Arabella replied. She had her hand on her chest, trying to catch her breath. "I'm fine."

"Let's go," Eva said.

"Yeah." Arabella nodded her head.

As Arabella was following Eva out of the locker room, she noticed something shiny on the locker room floor. She bent down to see; it was a necklace. She picked it up and examined it. It was an antique locket. She opened it, and she saw a picture, but she couldn't make out who it was. She placed the necklace in her pocket, then walked out of the locker room.

Later that night, Arabella is sitting on her bed, looking at the necklace. She placed the chain on the nightstand and went to sleep.

Arabella wakes in the same room as before; only this time, there is a bassinet in the room. She could hear a baby cooing. She looks over by the window and sees the figure man standing there.

"You, again." She said. "I'm starting to think that the only way I can talk to you is when I'm sleeping."

"Patience Arabella." He told her. "We will meet. You will soon know the truth."

She walked towards the bassinet and saw a baby boy. The baby looked up and smiled at Arabella. She placed her hand on the baby, and suddenly a wave of energy rushed through her. She fell to the floor and slowly went unconscious.

"I'll see you soon." Arabella heard the man say. Arabella wakes up and quickly grabs her journal to write down her dream. It was weird, she thought. She felt a connection when she touched the baby as if she knew exactly who the baby was. She places her journal in the nightstand drawer, and she quickly gets ready for school. And before going downstairs, she grabs the necklace and puts it on.

"Good morning." She said as she walked into the kitchen.

"Good morning-" Her father stops talking and looks at the necklace around her neck. "Where did you get that?"

"Oh, I found it yesterday after school." She explained.

"Lucia, honey," Tom said. "Look what Bell found."

"It's beautiful," Lucia said. "You're wearing it to school?"

"Yeah. I don't think it belongs to anyone." Arabella responded. "I have to go." She grabbed a piece of toast from her mom's plate, kissed her parents goodbye, and walked out of the house.

"Have you hung out with Julian yet?" Noah asked Maisie. He was leaning against the lockers.

"Arabella has," Maisie answered. "They went to the bar for dinner."

"Really?" Noah asked.

"Yeah, why do you care?" Maisie asked him. She closed her locker and adjusted her purse strap on her shoulder.

"She's like a sister to me." He explained. "I don't want her to get hurt."

"You and me both," Maisie said, taking Noah's hand. "I don't think the last conversation you had with Bell gives you any room to decide. My sister is capable of handling herself."

"I apologized. And it turned out that I was right." Noah justified.

"I know, but Bell doesn't need an older brother right now. She needs a friend." Maisie said.

Noah let out a sigh.

"Come on." She said, pulling him in the direction of their class.

Arabella sees Julian, and they both still haven't spoken to one another. Her life can finally go back to normal without him trying to ruin it with his excellent charm. "We are going to have to tell her eventually," Scott said to Eva.

"I know, but she has a lot on her plate," Eva said, kissing Scott's neck.

"She needs to know that her two best friends are in love with each other," Scott said, pushing Eva back. "We have to tell her."

"Okay," Eva said. "I'll tell her before the eclipse. Now can we please go back to kissing?"

Scott pulls her close to him and begins kissing her heavily.

"And we have to find a new place to meet. The janitor's closet is getting cramped." Scott said with a laugh.

Eva starts to laugh as well while she's kissing him.

"Agreed." She said.

Tom was sitting in his office with his face in his hands. Flashbacks of when Arabella and Maisie were younger flooded his head. They were innocent back then; they still were. Tom and Lucia have always tried to protect them the best way they knew how. And if that meant helping their daughters forget what happened to them, that was the price that Tom was willing to take over again.

"Mr. Holloway, your wife is on line one." Jennifer, his secretary, said after knocking on the door.

"Thanks, Jennifer," Tom said. He pressed the one on the keypad and picked up the phone. "Lucia."

"Tom," Lucia cried. "How did Arabella find the necklace?"

"I don't know. I thought we burned it." Tom said.

"He's coming for her," Lucia said. "I can feel him."

"Lucia, I'm going to give her a call," Tom told her. "She'll know what to do. I'll talk to you later."

Tom?" Lucia said.

'Yeah?" He asked.

"We can't keep running." She said. She hung the phone up.

Tom stared off into space before finally getting the courage to call the one person that started this mess. His mother.

"Tom, what is it?" His mother said.

"We have a problem," Tom told her. "He's coming."

"I'll be there soon." His mother said.

Tom puts the phone down and looks down at the police reports that were still on his desk. He didn't see it, but he grabbed his glasses, put them on, and then looked at the pictures again. He notices that each person had bite marks on the neck and wrist. The bites didn't look like animal bites. They were fang marks. Tom quickly realized that He was coming for her, but he left a message with the bodies he killed.

Tom reaches for the phone and dials the police station.

"Detective Schultz, how may I help you today?" a man asked on the other end of the phone.

"Schultz, it's Mayor Holloway," Tom said.

"Oh, hi, Mr. Holloway. Good thing you called. I just wanted to say that Beth and I appreciate you and your wife giving us the oatmeal cookies recipe. Beth's parents loved them." Detective Schultz said.

"Anytime. Shultz, I called in a serious manner. Is Fred in?" Tom asked.

"He just left to talk to Gilbert's family. By the bridge, their son's body was found." Schultz responded.

"Is he the latest victim?" Tom asked.

"As of now," Schultz replied.

"When he gets in, can you have him come to my house? There is something I want to discuss with him." Tom asked.

"Sure thing Mr. Holloway," Shultz answered.

"Thanks, Schultz," Tom said. He placed the phone on the hook.

Days passed, and Arabella and Julian haven't spoken to each other. It was almost as if they didn't know each other. She felt discouraged to talk to him; instead, she would sit outside with Eva and Scott and watch him. Everywhere she went, he was there. Staring at her from afar. Although it made her uncomfortable, she felt like he was protecting her in his creepy way. And that made her feel good.

Julian wanted to talk to her. He was longing for their conversations. But he couldn't risk her getting hurt or worse. Every day he watched her. I watched her walk home with Eva. I watched her go to sleep. He loved watching her, and with his family gaining close to the newborn vamp, he couldn't help but think that he wasn't going to see Arabella ever again when he leaves.

Maisie walked into the bathroom with her towel in one hand and her phone in the other. She turned on the shower, took off her slippers, and looked at the pictures that Noah sent her. He showed her ideas of what they could be for Halloween; she laughed at some and felt her body cringe for the rest. She placed her phone on the bathroom sink counter, took off her robe, and got into the shower.

When Maisie stepped out of the shower, she grabbed her robe and looked up, and screamed. She hadn't screamed that loud before since she was a child. She looked at the mirror; the words Don't Drink were written in the steam on the mirror.

"Maisie." Arabella came rushing into the bathroom. She saw her pale sister standing motionless in front of the mirror.

"Look." Maisie gestured to the mirror.

Arabella looked at the mirror and read the words. She quickly wiped the mirror with her hand.

"What does that mean?" Maisie asked her sister.

"Maisie, something is going on, but I'm not sure what it is yet," Arabella answered.

"Is everything alright?" Their dad asked, knocking on the bathroom door.

"Yes," Arabella said loudly. "We are fine."

"Maisie, I need you to trust me." Arabella looked back at Maisie. "Has there been anything strange going on lately?"

"Just yesterday, I was waiting for Noah, and I felt like someone was watching me." She replied. "Bell, what is going on?"

"I don't know, Mai. But I intend to find out." Arabella answered.

"One thing I know is when one of us feels something, never doubt it," Maisie said.

"A twin intuition," Arabella said.

Arabella walked into her room and sat on her bed. She looked down at the locket; she noticed that the picture was becoming visible to her, but she still couldn't make out the photo. Things were happening, and Arabella wanted to know the truth. She couldn't go to sleep that night, but somehow she managed.

"Fred." Tom greeted him at the front door. "Come in."

"Schultz said you wanted to see me," Fred said.

"Yes. I heard you were at Gilbert's house. I heard he was the latest victim." Tom said. "Have you found anything at the crime scene?"

"Unfortunately not. We are still looking. The only thing consistent with all the victims is that animals killed them. We did find that Gilbert put up a fight, unlike the other victims. He has DNA under his fingernails. We are running it through our system. We won't know more until tomorrow." Fred answered. "How is Arabella holding up?"

"She is doing okay, considering," Tom answered. Arabella was at the foot of the steps listening in on her dad's conversation with Fred. She didn't know that Gilbert was found dead. She hardly knew him, but the conversations she did have with him were sweet to her. He was a quiet one even when he graduated high school. She walked back to her room and climbed back into her bed. She had made up her mind that she was going to pay her respects to Gilbert's family.

"Tom, the guys at the station thought you could say something to lift the town's spirits with everything that has happened next week during the eclipse watch. The town needs to know that you will find out who is doing this and put everyone's hearts at ease." Fred said.

"Of course, Fred," Tom said.

"I have to get going now," Fred said. "I'll keep you updated."

"Goodnight." Tom walked Fred out.

Tom closed the door behind Fred and started walking to the kitchen. As he was walking, there was a knock on the door.

"Did you forget something, Fred-" Tom stopped when he saw his mother standing on the porch.

"Tom." She said. "Aren't you going to let me in?"

Arabella walked downstairs; she was on her phone, texting Eva. Eva told her that she had something to say to her and that they should talk. She looked up, and she thought about Boston. She hadn't got a chance to tell her parents that she got accepted to the university. But she wasn't sure if she would go with everything happening in the town. Suddenly she heard voices coming from the kitchen. She walked in and saw her grandmother sitting at the counter, drinking her coffee. "Gram?" Arabella said. "What are you doing here?" She placed her phone in her pocket.

"Good morning, everyone," Maisie said, stopping in the kitchen doorway. "What are you doing here, Gram?"

"Is that way to speak to your favorite and only grandmother?" Mildred said, opening her arms.

"No," Maisie said, smiling.

The girls both walked over to Mildred and hugged her.

"We are just surprised that you are here," Maisie said.

"Well, I just came to visit my beautiful granddaughters," Mildred answered.

"Your grandmother made her favorite tea," Lucia said. "You both should try some." Lucia poured the tea into two coffee cups and slid the cups across the counter for the girls.

Maisie looked at Arabella, and they both realized what the writing on the mirror meant.

"I have to get to practice," Maisie said.

"Yeah, and I have to meet with Eva and Scott to discuss the fundraiser," Arabella told them. "Will we see you guys at the eclipse tonight?"

"Um..of course," Tom responded.

"Alright. It's good to see you, Gram." Arabella said. Maisie and Arabella walked out of the kitchen, grabbed their purses, and left the house.

"That was weird, right?" Maisie said, glancing back at the kitchen window. She could see her grandmother watching her. She waved goodbye, and they both started walking to school.

"Very." Arabella agreed. "You don't think the tea is what the writing in the mirror meant, do you?"

"Bell, I don't believe in coincidences. One minute we both see the writing and suddenly Gram is here, and she makes her famous tea." Maisie noted.

"Whatever is in the tea, we can't drink it," Arabella told her. "Can't believe I'm saying this, but whoever wrote that on the mirror is trying to warn us about something. We need to be careful," she added.

"They will try to get us to drink the tea again," Maisie added. "Bell, I'm scared."

"Me too, Mai," Arabella said.

"Hey, look," Maisie said, pointing to Gilbert's house. There were police cars in the driveway, and a few people from the town were coming in and out of the house.

"I overheard dad talking to Fred last night. Fred said that Gilbert was attacked by an animal and killed." Arabella informed her.

"We should go in and say something," Maisie suggested.

Arabella nodded and followed Maisie up the driveway to the front door. The door was unlocked, and the girls walked in. While Arabella went to speak to Gilbert's dad, Maisie saw Gilbert's mother sitting in the living room, comforted by the town's people. She walked in and waited for her turn to say her condolences.

"Maisie, is that you?" Gilbert's mother asked.

"Yes, Mrs. Murphy," Maisie answered, sitting next to her on the couch. "Arabella and I just came to say we are sorry. We loved Gilbert very much."

"I know both of you did." She said. She wiped her tears with her tissue and then placed her hand on top of Maisie's. Suddenly Maisie felt weak. She saw blurry images of a man talking to Mrs. Murphy. He was somehow making her forget something awful. She quickly pulled away, apologized to Mrs. Murphy then promptly stood up.

She rushed out of the house, and Arabella had to run to catch up. Maisie bent over to catch her breath. Something was happening, and she didn't know what.

"Mai?" Arabella said. "What happened?" She placed her hand on Maisie's back.

"Bell, I saw something," Maisie replied. "It was like, I was there or something. Like I could see what happened in the past." She explained.

"What are you talking about?" Arabella asked, confused.

"Mrs. Murphy touched my hand, and it was like I was forced back to the night it happened," Maisie responded. "I don't think it was an animal that killed Gilbert."

"We need to find another way to get them to drink the tea," Mildred told Tom and Lucia. "They absolutely cannot remember what happened to them."

"We can't force it down their throats. They are older and asking questions." Tom mentioned.

"We need to do something," Mildred said. "Put some of the tea in the thermos and give it to them at the eclipse tonight. I heard it's supposed to get cold."

"And if they don't?" Lucia asked.

"We will prepare for the worse," Mildred replied. She finished drinking her coffee and went upstairs.

Tom and Lucia both looked at each other. Tom knew Lucia was frightened. So was he. He couldn't believe it had come down to this. Lucia walked over to Tom and started to cry. They were protecting their daughters as he saw it.

At school, Julian saw Arabella walking in the hall with Eva. They stopped at Arabella's locker and started talking. He wanted to walk to her and explain the reason why he wasn't speaking to her. It must've hurt her just as much as it hurt him.

"I wanted to tell you something." He heard Eva say.

"What is it?" Arabella asked, placing her purse in her locker.

"I'm just going to come out and say it," Eva said. "Scott and I are dating."

Julian watched as Arabella looked at Eva with joy. "Eva, I'm happy for both of you." Arabella smiled. "Really? You're not mad?" She asked. "Scott wanted to tell you, but I was holding it off. We've been friends since grade school, and I felt it was only right for me to tell you."

"I'm happy for you both, honestly," Arabella said again.

Eva hugged Arabella, and they both smiled as they walked to class. Julian saw Arabella sitting at the biology table, scanning the textbook. He walked over to her and sat down.

"Hey." He whispered.

Arabella turned to him and looked back at the textbook.

"You and I don't talk for two weeks, and then suddenly the only thing you can say to me is hey. Unbelievable." She said.

"I'm sorry," Julian said.

She looked at him, looked into his eyes. He felt like she was looking into his soul (if he had one).

"I can tell you mean it, so that's why I'm letting you off the hook." She told him.

"I do apologize for taking you home and not talking to you afterward. Something came up in my family, so I didn't know if I could trust you." Julian explained. Why would he lie? He could've told the truth or at least a part of the fact. He's mixed in something terrible, and he didn't want to cause any trouble to her. Anything other than what he just told her would have sufficed.

"Can you?" She asked. She leaned in closer to him.

"Can I?" He repeated, confused.

"Can you trust me?" She asked.

"I haven't decided yet." He smiled.

They both laughed. Julian closed his eyes; he missed hearing her laugh. He felt whole again. After class, Julian walked Arabella to her locker.

"Are you going to watch the eclipse tonight?" She asked him.

"Yes. My family and I will be there. I think they would enjoy the interaction with the town." He answered. "Will I see you there?"

"Yes." She smiled. In the distance, at the end of the hall, Arabella saw someone. It looked just like Tessa. There was no way she was dead. "Would you excuse me?"

"Yeah, of course." Julian nodded. He watched her walk away from him and make her way down the hallway. Arabella couldn't believe what she just saw. Was her mind playing tricks on her?

"Bell, where are you going?" Maisie called out. "Be right back." She followed Arabella down the hallway. When Maisie finally caught up to Arabella, she was in a chemistry classroom. Maisie watched as her sister looked around, trying to find something.

"Bell?" Maisie said. "Are you alright?"

"Mai, I saw her," Arabella answered.

"Who?" She asked. "Who did you see?"

"Tessa," Arabella replied.

"Are you sure?" She asked. "She died seven months ago." She walked towards her sister.

"I'm not crazy," Arabella whispered.

Tessa watched as Arabella and Maisie left the classroom. She smiled at the fact that Maisie didn't believe her sister. She walked out of the closet and looked out the window. She saw Arabella and her friends talking and laughing. Tessa's facial expression quickly changed to anger. They left her for dead, and those stupid doctors told her family that she was killed. The only reason Tessa came back was so she could kill Arabella. Make her pay for what she did. Tessa wanted to kill all the people that

Arabella loved, and only then would Tessa feel complete.

Arabella and Maisie were at home getting ready to watch the eclipse. Arabella was nervous. She wanted answers to what was happening to her. She just wanted someone to explain to her whether or not she was crazy. She looked down at the locket and then saw that picture was the same. She still couldn't see who it was. Arabella grabbed her coat and her phone and then went downstairs. Maisie and Noah were waiting for her in the living room.

"I'm ready," Arabella said.

"Well, let's go then." Maisie smiled. She grabbed her sister by the arm, and they left to watch the eclipse.

Ten minutes later, the three of them arrived at the bridge. The bridge had brought terrible memories back to Arabella. She shook it off and forced a smile. As Arabella saw everyone from the town gathering and drinking, she couldn't help but look for Julian. It surprised her. How badly she didn't want to look for the guy who pretended as if she didn't exist for two weeks, she couldn't help it.

As the sun set, everyone from town gathered around Arabella's dad to hear him speak.

"I know these few months haven't been easy, and the past few days aren't making them any better. I want to tell you that we will find killing our neighbors, friends, and teachers. I promise to you all that I will stop at nothing." Tom shouted into the megaphone. "Let us remember today is a good day. We are celebrating something good. With this special moment here with all of you, I know the goodwill outweighs the bad." He finished.

Everyone clapped and then started preparing for the eclipse. Arabella watched as everyone placed their glasses on and looked at the sky. Just as Arabella was putting her glasses on and everyone was beginning to stand still, someone bumped into her, almost knocking her down. A rush of energy she felt in her dream hit her. As she tried to maintain her bearing, she quickly turned around and saw a tall figure man heading toward the forest. She pushed through the crowd trying not to lose the mysterious man.

"Bell," Her mother stepped in front of her. "it's quite cold out, isn't it?"

"Just a little bit," Arabella answered. She was trying to get past her mother, but her mother wasn't moving.

"This will keep you warm." Her mother tried handing her the thermos.

"Mom, Eva needs me at the refreshment table." Arabella lied. "I have to go." she quickly slid past her mother, leaving her speechless.

"Have you seen them before?" Mildred asked Tom. She pointed to a group of people that were standing off to the side.

"No, I haven't," Tom answered. They both walked over to the family. "Hello. I'm Mayor Holloway, and this is my mother, Mildred. I don't think we've been properly introduced."

"Hi, I'm Caroline. This is my daughter Isla and my son Julian." Caroline said.

"You must be around my daughters' age. Both of them go to high school; you've probably seen them. Arabella and Maisie." Tom said, looking at Julian.

"Nice ring, you have there." Mildred looked down at Isla's silver ring. "May I ask, where did you get it?"

"This old thing. It's been in the family for years." Isla answered.

"We better get back," Tom said. "It was a pleasure to meet you all."

Tom and Mildred walked away.

"I saw that ring before," Mildred said. "There's going to be a problem."

"Who was that?" Edmund asked Caroline.

"The mayor and his mother. Came to say hello." Caroline replied, keeping her eyes on Mildred as they were walking away.

Arabella ran down the forest, searching for the man. She looked behind what seemed like several trees in search of him. She didn't have any luck. As Arabella turned to walk away and head back to the bridge, she felt a gust of wind behind her. She slowly turned around and saw a very tall man standing there. He was thin but muscular. He had dark straight short brown hair. Arabella slowly walked towards him and noticed that he had fair skin. His eyes were clear hazel that could melt just about anyone who looked at him. He was wearing a tight-fitted black shirt and jeans. He was the most handsome man she had ever laid eyes on.

"Arabella." He said softly.

The way he said her name made her knees grow weak.

"Do you know who I am?" He asked, walking towards her; she took a step back.

"Arabella." She heard her mother yell.

"Do I know you?" Arabella asked him. "Besides from my dreams. Who are you?"

"My name is-"

"Killian." Her mother said behind her.

Arabella turned around and saw her mother and the rest of her family with worry in their eyes.

"You know him?" Arabella asked her mother.

"Bell, come with me and we will tell you everything," Tom said.

"It's you," Mildred said.

"It's you as well," Killian said. "You've been living among them trying to pretend like you are something you're not." He added.

"Can someone please tell me what is going on?" Arabella yelled.

"I've seen you before," Maisie said.

"How?" Lucia snapped.

"The vision I had when Bell and I were at Murphy's house." She looked down at the ground and then up at Killian.

"I wanted you to," Killian explained. "You've been hiding her from me." He looked at Arabella's family. Killian crouched down and then drew his fangs out.

"No." Arabella stepped in front of him. She didn't know what was happening or how to comprehend that Killian had fangs coming out of his mouth.

"Arabella," Lucia said. "Don't."

"I'll go with you; just don't hurt my family," Arabella told Killian.

"Bella, don't go." Tom said

"I'm going to be fine." She said, keeping her eyes on Killian.

Arabella took Killian's hand; he picked her up then they were gone.

After twenty minutes of him running, Arabella didn't feel like she had to be nervous. She was the calmest she had been in a long time. Killian stopped running, put her down then started walking.

"Where are you going?" Arabella asked, following him.

"Arabella." He said.

"Why do you say my name like that?" She asked. "Like what?" He stopped and looked at her.

"Like you have something to tell me, but you don't want me to be frightened." She answered.

"All the years I have known you, you're still the same." He said.

"Years?" She repeated the word. "What do you mean?

"I'm not what you think I am. Julian isn't what you think he is." He began to say.

"How do you know Julian?"

"I've been- "

"You've been here watching me the whole time?"

"He's not what you think he is."

"And what's that? An overly possessive peculiar human being?" She said.

Killian chuckled.

"Arabella, we were set to marry." He bluntly told her.

"I don't believe you." She said. "Prove it."

Killian threw his head back, walked to her, and forcibly pulled her closer to him. He then bent down and kissed her. When he felt her soft lips, it was like he didn't miss anything. She tasted like warm peppermint. He could feel her heartbeat beat steadily; he knew he had her. Her warm body pressed against his made his body seem less cold. All the times he was searching for her began to suddenly vanish as she put her arms around him and pulled him tighter to her. He felt like his soul was open; he could see the colors of a rainbow. The sweetness and softness of her lips would haunt him for the rest of his days. He wanted more of her.

Flashbacks of what Killian said to Arabella came flooding her head. When she finally pulled away from him, she opened her eyes and looked up at him. He was already looking down at her. He was even more beautiful up close. But she remembered; she remembered everything.

BEGIN FLASHBACK:

"One. Two. Three." Arabella counted. "Four. Five. Ready or not, here I come." She pushed back from the tree and began to walk, searching for her sister. She adjusted her hat and began looking behind several trees and logs. She noticed that there was a stream flowing down to their home. She followed it; she noticed her sister's coat sticking out from behind one of the bushes. She carefully walked towards it. "Got you." She said. Her sister screamed and started laughing.

"Now you go hide," Maisie said.

Arabella started running to find a good hiding spot. She slipped on the mud and fell down the hill.

She sat up and brushed off the mud from her stockings.

"Are you alright, Miss?" a man asked her.

Arabella looked up and saw a man dressed in a British uniform walking towards her.

"Yes," Arabella answered. "Who are you?" She stood up.

"My name is Killian." He replied.

"You're fighting with the British army?" She asked. "Yes." He responded. "May I ask, what is your name?" He asked.

"I'm not supposed to talk to strangers." She told him. "We aren't going to be strangers if you tell me your name." He said. He walked closer to her.

"Arabella." She smiled at him.

"Ready or not, here I come." She heard Maisie yell. "Who is that?" Killian asked.

"My sister Maisie. We are playing, hide, and seek." She answered. "I better go hide." She started walking up the hill.

"Arabella?" He said.

"Yes." She turned her head to look at him.

"Will I see you tomorrow?" He asked.

"Yes." She replied. She continued to walk up the hill and went to hide.

Days quickly turned into weeks. Weeks turned into months. And months into years. Every day, Arabella found herself in the woods talking to Killian. From sunrise to sunset, she was in his company. As they talked for hours, she grew very fond of him. He was charming, and he had a way with words.

"Arabella, it has come to my attention that I haven't been frank with you," Killian stated.

"About what?" Arabella stopped walking, walked to the stream, and grabbed a white rock. She washed off the dirt that was on the rock and walked towards Killian. "You amaze me." He smiled.

"For you." She handed him the rock. "What did you want to tell me?" She asked, placing her hair behind her ear.

"Arabella," He began to say, "we've spent quite some time together. I watched you grow. Believe me when I say that, I am in love with you." He finished.

"I love you too, Killian." She smiled at him. She started walking past him, placing her hand on the trees and the leaves, feeling it on her fingertips.

"No, Arabella." He quickly ran in front of her. "I'm in love with you. From the first day, I met you."

Arabella's face grew quizzical. She stared blankly at him while he turned away from her. Her body grew still.

"I have been in love with you since I first laid eyes upon you. There is nothing good about me. Then you came along, the love you have for nature and animals; I knew fate brought us together. You're good. You have a good heart." He said. He didn't turn around.

"Killian." She said softly. "Look at me."

He turned around, and she gasped. She saw that his eyes were red. It was the first time she felt terrified of him.

"Killian, your eyes." She stepped back.

"This is who I am." He said, walking towards her. He grabbed her wrist and squeezed them tightly. "A vampire. I survive on the blood of humans."

"Killian, you're hurting me." She said. She tried pulling away from him.

Killian let her go and threw her back. She lost her balance and fell. When Arabella looked up, he was gone. She threw her back on the ground and started crying. She was probably crying for hours because when she looked up, it was nightfall. She stood up and looked around, hoping to see him coming from behind a tree. Nothing.

"Killian." She yelled.

He didn't come.

"Killian." She shouted again. She started running through the woods, searching for him. Then she stopped running. He wasn't coming back. She started crying again. She wondered why she was crying so much. Maybe it was the fact that, deep down, she was in love with him. She didn't care what he was. She just wanted him next to her. "Killian, I'm in love with you too. I don't care what you are. Just come back to me."

There was a cold gust of wind that blew behind her. "I'm here." He said.

Arabella turned around and saw him standing there, helpless. She picked up her dress and ran to him. She jumped into his arms and kissed him. The sweet taste of her lips made Killian grow weak. Breathing, his cold breath warmed her soul. At that moment, they both felt that only they existed. Time grew still as her lips pressed against his. He felt fireworks going off in his body with a mix of

Pandora's box effect. The connection they both possessed at the moment only intensified. The only thing he could focus on was how soft she felt. Heat rose from her body as they kissed. He gently pulled away to glance at the peak of her before he claimed her mouth again. He felt her body tingling with pleasure and excitement.

He finally pulled away to look down at her. She closed her eyes, and he gently rubbed her lips with his thumb before kissing her for the last time.

"I love you, Killian." She whispered. She placed her head on his chest, savoring their last moments together.

"I love you too." He said.

"I have to go now." She told him.

"Before you go," He began to say. He pulled out a handkerchief from his coat pocket, unfolded it, and a silver ring lay in his palm. "Arabella Maria Holloway, would you do me the honor of becoming my wife?"

"Oh, Killian." She cried. "Yes." She held her hand and watched as he slid the ring on her finger. He stood up, and he kissed her again.

Arabella opened the door to the cottage home and quietly walked towards the steps that led to Maisie, and she slept.

"Where have you been?" Her father asked, coming from the bedroom. Her mother was standing next to him.

"I was with Killian," Arabella answered.

"Oh, heavens." Her mother squealed. She rushed to Arabella and lifted her hand. Both of her parents saw the ring that was on her finger.

"I'm engaged," Arabella stated.

"Without my approval?" Her father said.

"I didn't know I needed your approval." Arabella snapped.

"You will bring that boy here in the morning." Her father demanded.

"We will discuss this in the morning." Her mother said.

Arabella and Killian walked to the cottage; her hand was clenched on his arm. He placed his hand on top of hers and then smiled.

"It'll be alright." He said.

Arabella opened the door, and they both walked inside. Her parents were at the table drinking tea.

"Mother. Father. This is Killian Winter." Arabella introduced him to them.

"It's a pleasure to meet you." Her mother hesitantly said. "Please have a seat."

Both Arabella and Killian sat down across from her father.

"It's a pleasure meeting both of you. It's wonderful seeing where Arabella spent-"

"Let's get one thing straight. I disapprove of this marriage. We both know what you are. Do you think you can honestly tell me that you can protect our daughter? Or when you get hungry, you won't see my daughter as a meal?" Her father interrupted him. "I have two daughters I need to protect. If you two continue this, it'll bring damnation to us all." He added. "Father." Arabella snapped.

"I think it's best you go and never come back." Her father told him.

"No." Arabella cried.

"It's okay." Killian turned to Arabella and kissed her. "Don't forget me," he whispered in her ear.

"Never." She whispered back.

"What I am has nothing to do with my love for Arabella. I'm in love with her, and I always will be." Killian said. He stood up from the table and walked out.

"Arabella, we are just trying to protect you and this family." Her mother told her.

"The only one that was going to protect me was him." Arabella cried. She stood up from the table and went up the steps to her bed.

Killian opened the door to the Porch House, where The Council was located, and the bedroom where Killian spent most of his nights. As he headed towards the stairs, Demetri came from the other room and said, "The Council would like to see you."

"Can this wait until the morning?" Killian asked.

"No, it cannot," Demetri said.

Killian followed Demetri into the other room where The Council was sitting in their wooden thrones. The Council was made of four vampires. They were the oldest among all the vampires. There was Clive, the diligent one. In any situation, he always sought to see it through. Monty, the demented one. The other vampires were frightened of him as he always acted on impulse. Then there was Felix, the reticent one. It is said that he never spoke; instead, he nodded in agreement. Lastly, Hadriana. She was the one that created Killian. She was his master until she released him from her command several years ago. The hate Killian had for her was unbearable even for him. He hated her for turning him into a monster. Into someone who feeds on others, who doesn't age, and for witnessing his loved ones die before him.

"It has come to our attention that you've been spending quality time with a human," Monty said. "A human that you've come to fall in love with."

Killian turned around to look at Demetri, who could see the future. He turned and focused his attention on The Council.

"I did not know what I did outside of the walls, possessed your attention," Killian said.

"We've mentioned to you when you came that the decisions you make would reflect us and the vampire world," Clive said.

"You fell in love with a human. You put her world and our world in grave danger." Hadriana said.

"You must face the consequences," Clive added.

"Very well," Killian said.

"Or we could kill your human, and you will watch," Monty suggested.

"That won't be necessary," Killian told him. "She didn't do anything wrong. It is I who pay."

"It is settled then," Hadriana said. "You will be stabbed in the heart with a steak, and you will awaken when she has no memory of who you are.

While Killian was preparing for Hadriana to stab him in the heart, Arabella and Maisie came down the steps and saw their parents and grandmother sitting at the table.

"Arabella. Maisie." Their mother said. "There are things that cannot be explained, but we just want you both to know that we are protecting you."

"This is tea." Their father said. "It'll make you forget." "I don't want to forget," Arabella said. "I love him."

"I know you do. But I know that you do not want to put our family in danger." Her father said. "Drink the tea, and you'll forget."

"It'll be alright," Maisie said. She picked up the cup and took a sip.

"It's your turn, Arabella." Her grandmother said.

Maisie handed Arabella the cup, and she took it. Tears began to come down her face; then, she took a sip of the tea.

Killian was awakened just like The Council said he would. He quickly rushed out and ran to Arabella's cottage home as fast as he could. When he reached the cottage, he noticed that it was on fire. Flames were coming from all around the cottage and from the inside.

"Arabella." He yelled. He used superspeed to circle the house, hoping to find someone or anything. He finally went into the cottage, kicking the door in. He searched throughout the cottage until he saw a body lying on the wood floor. He noticed that it was Arabella. He bent down, held her to his chest, and started crying.

Killian carried Arabella's body out of the cottage and laid her on the ground. He began to dig; once the hole was large enough, he placed her body in and then piled the dirt on her body. He felt like he was burying himself. A piece of him was gone. He hated himself, but importantly he hated her parents. He wanted them dead. And he was going to stop at nothing to kill them. Present Day.

"I remember," Arabella said. "I remember everything."

"I never stopped searching for you," Killian told her. He had his hands on her waist.

"Killian, I'm so sorry." She cried. She put her hand on his chest. "You told me not to forget, and I did."

"It's okay." He raised her head then he kissed her again. "I see you found the locket." He grabbed the necklace and opened it. It was a visible picture of Killian. Then he pulled away, reached into his shirt, and pulled out a locket necklace. He opened it to show her; she saw a picture of her inside. She threw her arms around Killian, holding him tightly.

Arabella opened the door to her house and walked in. She saw her family in the kitchen.

"Hey," Tom said.

"We didn't think you were going to come back," Lucia said.

"I'm here for an explanation," Arabella said. "I want an explanation as to why you kept him from me?"

"Arabella, they were protecting you," Mildred said.

"Why does everyone think I can't protect myself?" Arabella asked.

"What did he tell you?" Tom asked.

"How we met. He proposed to me, and then you disapproved. Killian died, and when he came back, he found my body on the floor in a burning house." Arabella responded. "I thought I was crazy."

"Sweetheart, we were just doing what we thought was right," Lucia said.

"What else are you three not telling us?" Arabella asked. She and Maisie stared at the three of them.

"Your father and I are witches, and your mother has memory manipulation," Mildred answered.

"I was able to see in the past," Maisie said nervously.

"And me?" Arabella asked.

"We figured that when Maisie was able to see in the past, that your gift would've come," Lucia explained. "Don't worry."

"How old are we?" Maisie asked.

"Seventeen," Lucia answered.

"Really?" Maisie asked.

The three of them looked at one another and then at the girls.

"We are as old as Killian," Tom said.

"And here I thought it was just your good looks that made you look young Gram," Arabella said.

"Your grandmother cast a spell so we would stay like this," Tom explained.

As Arabella stood at the counter listening to every word they were telling Maisie and her, she wanted to speak to Julian. Now that she knew what he was, she felt he owed her an explanation.

Noah got out of his truck in front of the bar and walked inside. The bar was empty since everyone was watching the eclipse.

"Order for pickup," Noah said. He watched the waiter return to the kitchen, holding a brown paper bag. He handed the food to Noah; Noah gave the waiter the exact amount of money and walked out.

As he walked and was about to get into his truck, he heard a scream from the alley. He placed the food on his vehicle's bed and investigated the riot. He headed down the path and saw a woman kneeling and biting into a man. Noah saw a broken pallet next to a dumpster. He broke a piece off and began to proceed toward the woman. Once he was close enough and about to stab the woman, the woman quickly grabbed his wrist, kept her face hidden, then pushed him back. Noah landed on top of the dumpster. He promptly fell to the ground. He groaned as he tried to stand up. The woman vanished. Noah wobbled towards the man. He saw that the man was dead. Noah quickly dialed the police.

Police arrived; paramedics took Noah to the hospital. His parents had met him there and were in the room when the doctor checked his blood pressure.

"Can we have a minute with our son, please?" Noah's dad asked the nurse.

"Of course." She replied.

"What the hell happened?" His dad asked after the nurse left the room.

"I saw a vampire," Noah answered. "I don't think those animal attacks were just animal attacks."

"We have to find it and kill it before anyone else sees it." His mom said.

Suddenly, Tom's phone rings. He sees that it is Fred and picks it up.

"Tom," Fred quickly said. "I think you better get to the hospital. Quick."

"I'll be right there," Tom said. He hung up the phone. "That was Fred. I think he found another body."

"I'm coming with you," Lucia said.

"Me too," Mildred added.

"What about us?" Arabella asked.

"Stay here," Tom told her.

"I have to go see Julian," Arabella told her sister. She proceeded to walk out of the kitchen.

"I saw your Boston acceptance letter," Maisie said.

Arabella stopped walking and then turned around to look at Maisie.

"When were you going to tell me that you were accepted?" Maisie asked. "I didn't know you applied."

"I applied after the accident," Arabella told her.

"I thought we were both staying here after high school?" Maisie said.

"Then the accident happened. I didn't want to stay. You saw what happened when Peter saw me." Arabella said.

"Are you going to tell mom and dad?" She asked.

Arabelle thought about the question. She still wanted to go to Boston, but some of her wanted to stay. Killian was in her life now, and she didn't want to lose him by any means.

Julian was on his balcony thinking about Arabella. He couldn't stop thinking about her. He felt the presence of Isla and said, "What do you want?"

"Edmund went to see if he can track the new vampire down," Isla answered. "What are you doing up here alone?"

"Contemplating life." He answered. "Any idea who she is?"

"No, but-" She trailed off and closed her eyes. "She's here."

Julian and Isla quickly went downstairs. Caroline stepped away from the bar and watched Julian walk to the front door. He opened it just as Arabella was going to knock.

"Hey." He said.

"Hey," Arabella said. "May I come in? I need to talk."

"Yes, of course." He opened the door and watched her walk past him. "Arabella, this is my sister Isla and my mother, Caroline."

"Nice to meet you," Arabella said, ignoring the fact that Caroline looked like she could be her sister.

"You as well, dear," Caroline said, smiling.

"What did you want to talk about?" He asked.

"I need you to be honest with me," Arabella said. "Are you guys vampires?"

They all stared at her blankly.

"I met Killian. He told me you and he are the same." She said.

They didn't speak.

"He told me how he and I met." She added. She looked at the three of them. "Well?"

"Arabella-" Julian was interrupted by Isla.

"How do you know Killian?" She asked.

"I knew him," Arabella said. "To be completely honest, we were in love."

"Were?" Julian said.

"That part is still pretty blurry." She said. If she had to be honest with herself, even if she had images in her head of Killian, she still didn't know him. And he didn't know her.

"Whatever Killian said to you about us is true," Caroline said.

"I'm surprised that I didn't see this," Isla said.

"See what?" Arabella asked.

"Sorry. I can read minds. And Julian-well I'm just feeling a bit strange as to how I didn't see who you were." Isla responded.

Arabella's phone buzzed. She looked down and saw a text from Maisie.

Noah is in the hospital; I am going to go. It should be fine.

"Is everything okay?"Julian asked.

"Noah is in the hospital. I have to get back home." Arabella said.

"I'll drive you," Julian suggested.

"Thank you." Arabella smiled.

They both got into Julian's truck. He started the engine and drove out of the driveway. The car ride was silent as both wanted to speak, but neither knew what to say.

"Does anyone else know what you are?" She asked, breaking the silence.

"No," Julian responded.

"What's the real reason you are here in Toronto?" She asked.

"What makes you think there is a real reason?" He asked, glancing at her.

She looked at him and then answered, "I've been lied to my whole life, if there is a real reason, I want to know."

"My family has been tracking a new vampire from Louisiana. Lately, the newborn has been getting sloppy. Just a matter of time, we find it and kill it." Julian responded.

"How do you kill it?" She asked.

"Burning." He replied. "There's a lot to know from us, but first, get some sleep." He slows the truck down to a stop. He puts the car in park and then turns to look at her. She looks at her house and then at Julian.

"Are you going to be alright tonight?" He asked.

"Yeah. I'll be fine." She lied. She didn't want to tell him that everything she had learned tonight scared her, and she didn't want to be alone. But she needed to be alone. "Thank you." She leaned over to kiss him on the cheek. She moved back, then opened the door and got it. She walked to the front door, and before going in, she turned around and waved at him.

Arabella sent a text to Eva and Scott, letting them know that Noah was in the hospital. She walked to her room, grabbed her robe, and went to shower. Letting the warm water hit her body felt good. Ten minutes later, Arabella walked to her room with a towel squeezing the water from her hair.

Then there was a knock.

Arabella looked up and saw Killian by the window. She gasped and quickly went to open it.

"What are you doing?" She asked.

"I had to see you." He said.

"Come in before someone sees you." She said. She steps back and watches him climb through the window and close behind him.

"How are you?" He asked.

"Well, I just found out that the guy of my dreams is a vampire, I'm as old as you, and my family has supernatural powers." She said. "I'm feeling just peachy." She sat down on the bed and buried her face in her hands.

"Arabella?" He said, kneeling in front of her.

"What was I like?" Arabella asked when she picked her head up.

"When?" He answered.

"When you met me." She answered.

He stood up and sat next to her on the bed.

"You were this clumsy little girl who looked at the world differently than most people do. You loved to be outside, thanking every leaf, rock, water drop for being beautiful in an ugly world. You wanted to love and peace, so you never killed any animal." He explained. "What makes you think I'm the same girl you fell in love with?" She asked. She stood and started pacing around the room. "I mean, it sounds like me, but I don't know if it's me."

"I know what's in your heart." He said, grabbing her by the shoulders. "I will continue to love you." He said. She didn't say anything; instead, she exhaled.

"Arabella, we possess a connection, and I'm not going to let you go again." He told her.

"Killian." She said, smiling at him.

He kissed her softly on her forehead.

Atlas, Arabella felt relaxed. Despite everything she learned that night, she felt alleviated. Arabella agreed that she and Killian shared this magnetic chemistry that would intensify soon. She felt it in the pit of her stomach. In the moments when

Arabella is with him, she isn't terrified. She was relieved. Was it possible that Killian somehow lifted a weight off her shoulders? She had no idea that this was what she was missing. Eternal satisfaction, she felt.

Julian asked her if she was still in love with Killian, and maybe that was the one thing her parents couldn't get rid of; the love she possessed for him. Being with Killian at that moment made her realize that she was, in fact, in love with him. And she didn't need anyone telling her otherwise.

The next day, Noah was in his father's study with both of his parents, going over how they would get rid of the vampire in town, killing the natives. Noah's parents prepared him for this moment. Every day, his father would give him a lecture and an archery class on killing vampires. Noah was more than ready to put it to the test.

"You better get to school." Noah's dad said.

"No one must know about last night's attack." His mother told him.

"As of right now, they think it was an animal attack," Noah said.

"Let's keep it that way." His father demanded.

"I'll see you guys after school," Noah said. He kissed his mother on the cheek. "Later, dad." Noah grabbed his backpack and walked out of the study. He grabbed his keys and then walked out of the house.

Twenty minutes later, he arrived in the school parking lot. He saw Maisie and Arabella talking to Eva and Scott; Noah quickly got out of his car and jogged toward them. He fought against eminent loss

Maisie and frightened her; she panted and turned around, and she tossed her arms around him before kissing him.

"Are you okay, Noah?" Scott asked.

"A little bruised up, but I'm fine," Noah answered. "I didn't see you two after the eclipse."

"That's because we wanted to spend quality time," Eva responded. She kissed Scott on the lips.

"When did this happen?" Noah asked.

"A while now," Arabella said.

"And we are okay with this?" He asked jokingly

"I am." Arabella smiled.

"Me too," Maisie said in agreement.

Arabella could see Julian walking in their direction across the parking lot.

"Hey, I'm going to catch up with you guys," Arabella said. She began walking towards Julian.

"Are they a thing now?" Noah asked Maisie after watching Arabella leave.

"No, she has her eye on someone else," Maisie answered.

Noah kept his eyes on Arabella and Julian.

"Hey," Arabella said.

"Hey." Julian glanced at her.

"What's wrong?" She asked him.

He stopped walking and looked around, seeing if anyone was near them to hear what he had to tell her. "Isla was able to look into the mans' head, and the new vampire is a woman. She's new. And sloppy." Julian informed her. "Caroline was there in the town meeting this morning, and your dad issued a curfew."

"The fundraiser?" She asked.

"He's going to have every police officer in town here at the school." He answered.

"Are you going out to look for her?" She asked him. "No. Caroline and Isla are doing that. My dad is with yours going to the police station." He responded. "I'm here with you."

Arabella's face grew pale. She didn't know what to say.

"Unless you don't want me to be?" He asked.

"I do." She placed her hand on his arm. He looked down at her hand on his arm, and she quickly pulled away. "I'm glad you're here."

Julian placed his backpack in the locker in the locker room and grabbed his hockey jersey. As he was getting dressed, Noah noticed a tattoo covering a branding mark on his back.

"Nice tattoo," Noah said.

"What?" Julian said.

Noah pointed to the tattoo that was on Julian's back. "Oh, thanks," Julian said.

"How'd you get it?" Noah asked, putting on the shoulder pads.

"It was quite some time ago, and I don't remember," Julian answered. "I'll see you out there." He said, grabbing his hockey stick. He started walking towards the locker room doors.

"Yeah," Noah said.

Tom and Edmund were standing in front of the police report board. There were pictures of all the victims that were killed by animal attacks. Tom took the image of the latest victim and pinned it on the board.

"How did you know what we were?" Edmund asked.

"My mother spotted the ring your daughter was wearing. She recognized it. She knew a vampire that wore the same ring." Tom answered. "To prevent you from burning in the sun, right?"

"Mhmm." Edmund looked down at the ring he was wearing.

"Do you plan on staying in town once this is all over?" Tom asked him.

"It's a possibility," Edmund replied.

"Edmund, my daughter is in love with a vampire, and there is nothing I can do. My other daughter just discovered that she has gifts, and the town is in a frenzy because of these so-called animal attacks. I don't think I can shield them away from any longer from this world. But if you want to stay here, show me I'm making the right decision by letting you stay. Or I'll kill you myself." Tom said.

Edmund nodded, then focused his attention on the board.

The coach blew the whistle, and Julian smacked the puck across the ice. As he skated for an open area for one of the players to slide the puck to him, Noah skated fast in front of him and blocked him from retrieving it. Noah skated to the goal with the puck in front of him and shot toward the target. Each game they played, Noah aggressively pushed Julian out of his way so he could get the puck. Julian was starting to get angry. The coach blew his whistle for the game.

Julian watched as Noah skated off the rink and headed to the locker room. Julian went after him. "Noah," Julian yelled. "What the hell was that?"

"What was what?" Noah asked. He was sitting down, taking off his skates.

"What is your problem?" Julian asked him.

"Dude, it was just practice. Lighten up." Noah told him. "I was seeing if you could handle being on the team. We have our first game Friday."

"You're unbelievable, man," Julian said. He walked towards his locker and started changing.

Arabella was in the school's foyer with Eva and Scott hanging up posters for the fundraiser. She couldn't believe she and Maisie's birthday was almost here. She cringed at the fact that she was getting older and Killian would always look the same.

"School fundraiser?" A student said. "What are we raising money for?"

"The school trip the seniors take before winter break to give back to those who are less fortunate," Eva answered. "The fundraiser will be on Halloween in the gym. So dress up and bring your money."

"Oh, cool." The girl said. "I'll be there."

"What are you going to be for Halloween?" Eva asked Arabella.

"I haven't thought about it," Arabella answered. "I don't know if I'm going to go."

"You have to," Eva said. "Scott, can you please tell Bella that she has to come and experience high school?"

"Eva is right, Bella. When was the last time you had any fun?" Scott asked.

"I'll think about it," Arabella told them.

Arabella was sitting in her room when there was a knock on her window. She looked up from her homework and saw Killian smiling at her. She got off the bed, walked towards the window, and opened it. "You know normal people use the front door." She said.

"I know. I thought this was more romantic." He told her. He climbed into her bedroom and closed the window behind him.

"You're going to have to forgive them," Arabella said.

"I can't." He began to walk around the room.

"They were doing what they thought was best at the time," Arabella sighed.

"Arabella, I searched for you for decades. I thought you were dead. I will never forgive them for keeping you from me." He expressed.

Arabella sighed; she knew she wouldn't get through to him.

"My school is having a fundraiser on Halloween," She steered away from their conversation, "I was wondering if you want to come with me?"

"On your birthday?"

"Yeah." She confirmed. "You don't have to come. High school is probably not your scene."

"It would be my honor to accompany you." He smiled at her. "May I ask, why didn't you ask Julian?"

"What?"

"I have seen the way he looks at you and the way you look at him."

"Are you jealous?"

"No." He claimed.

She shouted, "I realize we are bound to be. I can feel it." She strolled forward, at that point halted, and left adequate space among them.

"I know." He whispered. "I have to go; I've been assisting Caroline and Isla with the search." He looked down at his phone.

"I don't want you getting hurt."

"I'm not." He walked close enough to her and placed a kiss on her forehead.

Arabella watched him walk to the window, open it and climb out. Before he jumped down, he gave her a warm smile. She watched him disappear in the dark. She walked towards her bed and threw herself down on it. As she lay there staring at the ceiling, her mind was racing. She was perplexed. Killian and Julian were both pleasant and empathetic. She couldn't help but pick between them in any way, shape, or form. However, she knew she needed to; she could not have the two of them.

"I think we could go as Bonnie and Clyde," Maisie suggested to Noah.

Noah got two bowls and spoons, "You realize the police murdered them, right?"

"Oh, come on." She begged.

"Alright." He grabbed the ice cream from the freezer. "It's always nice to hear voices in the kitchen." Noah's dad walked in and smiled.

"Hello, Mr."

"Oh Maisie dear, call me Gabriel." He said. "How is school?"

"It is good. We have this Halloween fundraiser at school, and we are going as Bonnie and Clyde." Maisie answered.

"That is lovely." Gabriel smiled. "Maisie, I need to have a word to my son, so if you'll excuse us. Noah, can I see you in the study, please?"

"Sure," Noah said, looking at Maisie. He handed her the bowl of ice cream and followed his dad into the study.

Maisie watched as they walked into the study, and Gabriel closed the sliding doors behind him.

"Are you sure you saw the branding mark on your friend Julian?" Gabriel asked.

"Yeah, he had a tattoo covering it., Noah responded.

"I don't think it is a convenience that you saw the vampire in the alley, and then you see the mark on your friend."

"What do we do?" Noah asked.

"We are going to have to kill him."

"Arabella and Julian have been growing close to each other," Noah informed him.

"Son, we are hunters. It's what we do."

"I'll do it at the Halloween fundraiser. There will be a lot of people there so that the police won't suspect a thing." Noah assured him.

Tessa Walsh. That was her name. It still is. Tessa was the most attractive girl in high school until Arabella and Maisie came along. Then suddenly, she became the girl who didn't matter. But it didn't matter to Arabella because she and Tessa became good friends. Now that Tessa thinks about it, the word good is an understatement. Arabella and Tessa became two peas in a pod. When you see one, you are bound to see the other girl. The two girls were inseparable. So this story about Tessa Walsh isn't your average story that made headlines; it was more profound than that. No, it was something more significant. Something is humane. And she remembers it like it was yesterday.

BEGIN FLASHBACK:

No one knows when they are going to die or let alone how they are going to die. But Tessa was less concerned about that. She just wanted to have fun; let loose, if you will.

Tessa was standing in front of Arabella's car with Eva and Scott. It was the first time Tessa had thought about going out since Landon and she broke up. (Landon was the center on the hockey team. He moved to New York after he graduated high school.) Tessa didn't take their break up well. She wouldn't eat or sleep, and she was always hearing her mother utter the words, "Quit your whining." Tessa felt like the quiet girl in school; she wanted someone to ask how she was doing. And maybe, she would feel less sad.

"Stop being a party pooper," Arabella said to Tessa. "Live a little."

"So Tessa, what do you say?" Eva asked. "Are you going to come with us and have the greatest night of your life, or are you going to go home?"

The three of them stared at Tessa for an answer. Then she smiled, and Arabella jumped for joy.

Let's ride," Scott said.

How was Tessa going to say no to that? Especially the three of them? Tessa smiled, letting them know she wanted to have fun. Even with all the drinking, Tessa just wanted to feel something. She didn't want to think about Landon or her mother not taking her pain seriously or anything else for that matter.

The four of them climbed into the car and started driving. The music was loud; neither could have heard what the other one was saying. Arabella ran through every stop sign in the town, and the other three cheered her on. Tessa grabbed one of the tequila bottles and then took a gulp. As Scott cheered her on, Tessa took another drink, not stopping until she practically spilled some of it on her leg. The four of them laughed and danced to the music.

Arabella drove the car in the direction of the bridge that separates the town from the city. As Arabella was driving, a bright light shone on Tessa's face. Tessa looked up and saw headlights. Tessa's body went numb, and the vehicle immediately struck the four of them.

The car spun in the direction of the bridge, and then everything grew silent.

Tessa remembers the sound of the car horn going off from the accident. She knew it was the end for her; she didn't fight it. Tessa felt pain, and then she didn't. Felt her body sink as if she was in the water; she was too far gone to get help.

The paramedics took Tessa to the hospital after announcing she was dead. There her parents and Tessa's brother came immediately after hearing the news. The doctor pulled the white sheet back; her mother became hysterical. Tessa's father let out a soft cry; he tried to comfort Tessa's mother. Peter, Tessa's older brother, quickly grew furious as he wanted to know who killed his little sister. The doctor stated that a car accident left the other three passengers injured. The doctor stood silently, letting the family grieve and wrap their minds around what had transpired. When Tessa's mother was able, she told her husband that she had seen enough and would like to take it home. Paul was the last to leave, but before he left, he bent down to Tessa and whispered that he loved her. Always.

It was silent in the morgue. Cold, and it smelled like the autoclave sterilized the equipment. Suddenly the drawer that was holding Tessa's body was opened. Roughly ten minutes later, Tessa's eyes opened.

She looked around, examining where she was. It didn't take her long to learn that she was in the morgue, but she realized she wasn't dead. Alive. But how? She remembered the vehicle that struck her. She remembered the headlights. How could she forget them? It was like a bright train light that she would never get out of her mind. Tessa slowly sat up, got off the drawer, and looked around the room.

"Finally, you're up." A voice said, coming from the darkness in the corner of the room.

"How am I here?" Tessa asked.

"All that will be explained, but what is important is that you are alive." The voice said, walking towards her.

It was a man. He was slim but stocky with broad shoulders, standing six feet tall; his hair was jet black and neatly combed. The man had smooth olive skin, and his lips were lush and narrow. As he walked closer to her, his eyes were wary soulless brown eyes. His clothes were fabulous and modest.

"Who are you?" Tessa asked.

"My name is Damien Pierre." He answered in his British accent.

Tessa took note of it and proceeded to ask him more questions. But before she could, she smelled something. It was somehow making her weak. She put her hand on her throat and looked at Damien.

"You smell that, don't you?" he asked.

"What did you do to me?" she asked, clinging to her throat. Her eyes grew red as she quickly ran across the room; Damien ran after her stopping her in her tracks. "You will get to feed soon." He told her. "Come with me."

Tessa followed (as if she had a choice) out of the hospital. Damien led her to an old brick building in the city. He explained what she was and that he had saved her life. Explain to her that something was intriguing about her that led him to make a rational decision. Tessa stood motionless on the pile of bricks; she didn't know how to react. Damien talked for hours. Tessa listened.

Could this be happening, she thought?

"It has come to my attention that we share a mutual enemy." he turned around to look at her.

"A mutual enemy?" she asked hesitantly.

"Arabella Holloway," How could Tessa forget? She is only in this predicament because of Annabel. Tessa's face grew angry.

"I'm not wrong, am I?" he walked closer to her.

"So what?"

"I'll let you kill her."

"Excuse me?" she asked. "How do you know her?" "You don't need to concern yourself with the details," he replied.

"How do I know that you aren't going to kill me instead?" she asked.

"If I wanted to kill you, I would have done it without any hesitation," he told her.

Tessa felt her body grow still, and before she knew it, she was mouthing the words, "I want her dead."

Later that night, Tessa couldn't fathom all that Damien said. She felt like she was in a nightmare and couldn't wake up. But Damien was right; Tessa wished for Arabella to die, for her to feel the pain that Tessa endured.

END FLASHBACK.

Tessa stood on the cliff, staring down at Evergreen Springs. She felt a cold chill blow behind her, and without turning around, she said, "Was starting to think you weren't going to show."

"And miss all the fun?" Damien stood next to her. Tessa turned to and looked at him; he was still the same. Not a gray hair or wrinkle in sight. Despite his being beautiful, there was a flaw. There was a scar below his ear. Tessa hadn't noticed it before, and she was frightened to ask.

"It's not polite to stare," he said.

"I'm sorry." she shifted her head and eyes toward the town. "If I ask, are you going to tell me?"

"No," he answered. "perhaps you should assert your curiosity elsewhere, with a gentleman in particular."

"If you are referring to Noah, I handled it."

"How can you be certain?" he asked. "His family comes from a long line of vampire hunters."

"I said it is dealt with."

As they both didn't say anything, Tessa continued to look down at Evergreen. She stood still, inhaling the cool breeze. Tessa could smell the sweet scent of human blood whisking through their veins.

She could hear various conversations throughout the town. The town she once knew became foreign to her. Tessa wanted to go back to that day when her life ended. She knew she was forever going to be in Damien's debt. Not that she isn't grateful for him bringing her back, but her life as Tessa Walsh died in the car. She is this monster that barraged on anything with a pulse.

The day was here—Arabella's eighteenth birthday. The day she couldn't wait for turned into a typical day; she couldn't wait for it to over. Arabella stared at herself in the mirror with her hair rollers in her hair; she glanced over at the pin-up a-line dress that Killian had bought her. She wondered what he was going to be tonight. As the idea of him dressed in anything but a shirt and jeans stayed in her mind, she put on the yellow dress, took her hair out of the rollers, running her fingers through her hair. Arabella gazed at herself in the mirror; she smoothed out her clothing; she was a 1950 pin-up girl. She let out a soft chuckle. Arabella then heard a knock at the door; it must be Killian.

"Could you get that?" she shouted from her room.

Tom walked to the front door and opened it. Killian was standing there in a 1950s military uniform.

"Tom," Killian said. "How are you?"

"Killian, it's always a pleasure to see you," Tom said. "I don't have to tell you to come in, do I?"

"I'm afraid not."

Killian steps past Tom, taking off his cap. He sees that there are portraits of Arabella and Maisie on the cupboard. He walks towards them, gaining a closer look. He smiles, seeing how young and beautiful his Arabella once was.

"Killian, you're looking well." Lucia walked towards Tom from the kitchen entrance.

"You as well, Lucia." Killian gave her a warm smile. "The only reason we are letting you be with our daughter is that we don't want to see her in any more pain," Tom told Killian.

"I must ask, how'd you do it?" Killian asked both of them.

"Cloaking spell," Tom answered.

"When did you know?" Lucia asked, stepping in front of Tom.

"The day she fell into the water in Paris. She was only eighteen. She couldn't swim, and I felt her." Killian explained. "I came for her, and it was like meeting her all over again. We ran away together, and she got pregnant. Then you both took her away from me."

"Is that true?" Arabella said from the stairs.

The three of them glanced up at her.

"The baby boy from my dream...that was our son?" she asked, walking towards Killian.

"His name was Archie," Killian informed her.

"How did he die?" she asked.

"I don't think that is important," Killian advised her.

"I want to know." she placed her hand on his arm.

"He drowned," Tom answered.

Arabella gripped Killian's arm.

"We better get going," Arabella said, looking up at Killian. "Maisie and Noah are at the school."

"We are going to the town hall," Lucia told them. "Happy birthday again, sweetheart," Tom said, kissing Arabella's head.

Arabella forced a smile.

Arabella and Killian walked out of the house, making their way to his car. Killian sensed that Arabella wanted him to explain himself, but he realized it wasn't the right time, nor did he think it ever would be.

"I know you are wondering why I didn't tell you about Archie," he spoke.

"How old was he when he died?"

"Three months."

Arabella didn't say a word for the rest of the ride. She quickly wiped a tear from her eye and gazed out the window.

They arrived at the school twenty minutes later; Killian parked his car and got out. He walked towards the passenger door and then opened it.

"Before we go in, I want to give you something," Killian said, reaching into his pocket. He pulled out a red rectangular box. He opened it, and inside was a gold chain with a charm on it.

"It's beautiful." she held out her wrist.

"Had this made when I first saw you."

"Thank you." she wrapped her hand around his neck, pulled him down to her, and kissed him.

"Happy birthday," he said, pulling back.

"There you are." a voice said behind Killian.

Killian and Arabella turned to look; Maisie and Noah were standing there. They dress as the notorious Bonnie and Clyde.

"Hey," Arabella said. "You two look great."

"So do the both of you." Maisie hugged her sister. "Noah, this is Killian." Arabella introduced him.

"How do you do?" Killian politely said.

Noah gave Killian a wry look.

"Did you bring it?" Maisie asked.

"Bring what?" Arabella asked.

"The fundraiser bowl," Maisie said.

"No. I completely forgot." Arabella said. "Killian and I will go back home to get it."

"Hurry," Maisie said.

Tessa stood in front of her family's home for fifteen minutes before walking towards the front door. She knew her parents had left to go to the town hall, and her brother was home alone.

She knocked on the door, waiting for Peter to answer. "Who is it?" Peter shouted.

Tessa didn't say a word. She was standing with her back to the door.

"I'm not passing out any candy," Peter said, opening the door.

Tessa turned around and said, "Hey, Pete."

"Tessa," he said.

"Are you going to let your sister in?"

"Of course. Come in." he opens the door wide so she can walk past him.

Tessa walks in and walks into the living room. Everything was the same when she died, not even a couch pillow out of place.

"Am I dreaming?" Peter asked. "How are you alive?"

"No," she responded, ignoring his question.

"I have to call mom and dad; they are going to be happy when I tell them you are alive."

"No. You can't." Tessa shouted. "No one must know I'm here."

"Are you in trouble?"

"Pete, remember when I fell off my bike, and you told me that you would do anything to protect me?"

"Yeah."

"I need your help." she pleaded.

"Anything?" Peter said, putting down his phone.

"I need your help to kill Arabella and her friends."

Meanwhile, at the school, Julian was walking towards the school gymnasium. He could hear distant chatter when he opened the door; the warm smell of caramel apples filled his nose. He could see everyone dressed in their costumes. He watched as many of the students came in through the gym's back door; the committee had set up events behind the gym. Julian quickly spotted Eva and Scott, who were dressed as police officers and an inmate.

"Have you both seen Arabella?" Julian asked.

"Maisie said she went back home to grab the fundraiser bowl," Eva answered. "By the way, who is Killian?" "How do you know Killian?" Julian asked.

"He's the one that drove her back home," she responded.

"They are friends." Julian lied.

"Seemed like they were more than friends," Scott added.

"We are going to walk around for a bit. Don't forget to donate." Eva said before she hurried off with Scott. Julian walked over to the punch bowl, poured the punch into a plastic cup then took a sip. It tasted bitter to him.

"Hey, man," Noah said next to him.

"Noah, let me guess?" Julian took a step back and examined Noah's costume. "Clyde. And that would leave Maisie as Bonnie."

"That obvious?"

"You could've fooled me."

"What are you dressed as?"

"Me," Julian answered. "I'm not big on Halloween." "Really?" Noah asked.

"Yeah." Julian looked around as more students were coming in. "I better go mingle."

"Yeah." Noah agreed. He watched Julian walk away and fade into the crowd.

Killian drove into Arabella's driveway and parked. He told her he would wait in the car while she went inside. He watched her run to the front door, unlock it and disappear in the dark.

Arabella knew precisely where the bowl was, but that wasn't the only reason she returned home. She had left her locket necklace hanging from her mirror in her room. She quickly ran upstairs to grab it.

Peter found a rock near the back door and managed to break the door glass with it. He reached in and unlocked the door. Peter looked around the kitchen. It was quiet. He walked stealthily to the staircase. "Killian, is that you?" Peter heard Arabella shout from the stairs. He hid in the closet that was under the stairs. Julian walked out of the restroom and made his way to the gym.

"You think you are so clever?" a voice said behind him. Julian turned around. Noah was standing there, clenching his fist.

"You know at first; I didn't notice," Noah said. "But when I saw your tattoo, I knew."

"It's just a tattoo, Noah."

"It's covering a brand mark," Noah said. "My dad told me about a different species and how everyone could tell they were different from others was by a brand mark. It's the same mark you have."

"Noah, that would make a good bedtime story," Julian said. "Let's get back to the gym." he turned to walk away.

"You're a vampire," Noah shouted.

Julian stopped walking.

"You're a vampire, and you can't stand there and tell me differently." Noah drew the wooden stake from behind him.

Julian looked down, then up at Noah.

"Noah, think about what you're doing," Julian tells him.

"I have. I come from a long line of vampire hunters. This is who I am."

"I'm older than you, Noah. So I'm a lot stronger than you."

"I still have to kill you." Noah sprinted to Julian, trying to stab him with the stake.

Julian dodged him with his superspeed forcing Noah to slam into the floor.

"You probably know the girl that was sucking her teeth into that poor man," Noah said, throwing his fist at Julian.

"I don't." Julian threw Noah against the lockers. "I'm not the enemy, Noah."

Noah looked up, and Julian was gone. Noah needed to find Julian before he caused more trouble.

Killian got out of his car, walked up the porch steps, and walked inside the house. He was wondering what was keeping Arabella so long. He walked to the kitchen to grab a bottle of water. When he took a sip of the water, he noticed from the corner of his eye that the back door was broken. He looked down and saw a rock that was used to break the glass.

"Hey, I thought I heard you," Arabella said joyfully. "We have to go," Killian told her. He grabbed her hand, and as they rushed to the front door, Peter came out of the closet knocking Killian and Arabella on their feet. Killian quickly stood up and carried Arabella to the kitchen.

"Peter, what are you doing?" Arabella said.

"Something I should've done a long time ago," Peter answered. He grabbed Arabella and began to choke her. Killian came behind Peter and bit him. He immediately pulled away, noticing that Peter had vervain in his veins. Killian stumbled backward, trying not to swallow the toxin. Arabella was growing weaker; she could barely breathe. She looked down at Killian, who was weak from seeking his teeth into Peter's neck.

"This is for my sister," Peter growled. His grip grew tighter around Arabella's neck.

Arabella saw Julian walk around the corner. She watched him look down at Killian and then back at her. "She's alive," Peter whispered in Arabella's ear.

Julian quickly placed his hands on Peter's head and cracked his neck. Arabella fell to the floor, gasping for air. She hurried to Killian.

Arabella stood Killian to his feet; they both thanked Julian.

"We have a problem," Julian informed them. "Noah is a vampire hunter. He knows."

"We have to go," Killian said.

The three walked out of the house and immediately stopped when they saw Noah getting out of his car. Arabella holds on to Killian, who can barely stand.

"I knew there were more of you," Noah said.

"Noah, please," Arabella begged.

"Arabella, step away from them. You don't know what they are."

"I do," Arabella said. "You don't have to do this."

"Yes, I do," he explained.

"Noah," Maisie yelled.

Noah turned and said, "Stay out of this, Mai."

"I can't let you do this," she said, walking in front of Noah. "We know exactly what they are."

Noah looked at them and placed the wooden stake inside his coat pocket.

"We have to get out of here," Killian said.

"Come on," Julian said. The three got into Julian's truck, leaving Maisie and Noah on the lawn.

"Are you coming?" Arabella asked her sister.

Maisie looked at Noah with tears in her eyes.

"I'm going with you," Noah said.

Noah and Maisie got into Noah's car and followed Julian.

Twenty minutes later, both cars pulled into the driveway. They all hurried and went inside.

"What is this?" Caroline asked. She looked down at Killian, still in pain.

"No time to explain," Julian told her.

"Take him to the basement," Caroline demanded. "Who might you be?" she asked Noah.

"Noah," Noah answered.

"A vampire hunter," Isla said.

"Do you know what you have done?" Caroline shot her eyes at Arabella.

"He's with us," Arabella informed them.

"If anything happens to my family, it will be in your hands," Caroline warned her. She followed Julian and Killian to the basement.

Two hours later.

Arabella was sitting in the chair next to Killian's bed. Her fingers were in his; she hadn't moved from that spot since Julian and Noah brought him from the basement. She was exhausted from everything that had happened. Arabella didn't know how much she could take.

"He will be fine," Isla said, coming into the bedroom. "How can you be sure?" Arabella asked.

"It happened to me as well."

"Right." Arabella looked at Killian; he was motionless. "Your sister is dating a vampire hunter, and you are bound to the oldest vampire," Isla noted.

"If you're trying to say something, just say it already." Arabella snapped.

"Did you think about every day you are going to get older, and Killian isn't? What happens when you have blood gushing out of you? Do you think he will be able to save you?" Isla asked.

"Killian would never hurt me," Arabella told her. "He loves me and I—."

"Don't tell me you love him too?" she interrupted. "There's no such thing as a human and a vampire being together. The Council won't stand for it."

"I'll convince The Council. I won't lose Killian."

"Just know this, he will always be a vampire," she said. She walked out of the bedroom.

Arabella looked down at Killian. Isla was right; there was no changing Killian. The only thing she could think of was that she had to change. It wasn't like the thought didn't cross her mind because it did. She wanted to be with Killian. Her heartbeat beats for him, and she knew that. Arabella knew what she wanted, what she needed. She needed Killian to change her. It was the only way they could be together.

Arabella stood in Julian's foyer, listening as everyone screamed at each other about what they should do after Peter tried to kill her. She couldn't put her friends and family in jeopardy again. But then again, what was she going go to do about it?

"He told me that she is alive." Arabella blurted out. Everyone stopped talking and looked at her.

"Peter came after me and tried to kill me. He was under the influence of Tessa." Arabella added. "We need to find her."

"We have to kill her," Noah added.

"No one is dying," Arabella stated.

"I know you want to be a hero for everyone, but right now is not the best time. Someone has to die. And since we all agree that it won't be the both of you." Noah looks at Julian and Killian. "My vote is on Tessa. She killed all those people."

"Hunter boy is right," Isla said. "She already caused too much damage in this town."

Noah scoffed.

"Is there something else, Hunter boy?" Isla asked. "Never thought I would be talking to a vampire." He said. "And it's Noah, by the way."

Isla rolled her eyes at him.

"How much I hate admitting this, but they are right, Bell," Maisie said.

"Maybe I can reason with her," Arabella told them.

"Do you think she wants to reason with you? She sent her brother after you. Look what happened to him." Noah snapped. "I'm not saying you have to be there when we kill her but know that it will happen."

"I agree," Julian said. "We need to draw her somewhere."

"In the meantime, we need to act as if she won." Noah looked at all of them.

"Arabella will stay here," Caroline suggested.

"I'll stay with you." Julian looked at Arabella. Arabella smiled.

"I'll let mom and dad know." Maisie grabbed her phone and walked into the kitchen.

"In the meantime, don't draw attention to yourself," Noah told her.

"I have to go check on Killian." Arabella softly said. Arabella opened the bedroom door; Killian stood up, putting on his shirt. She knew he listened in on their conversation downstairs. She closed the door and walked towards him.

"I know," Arabella said, walking towards him. "Everything will be fine." she placed her hand on his cold chest, hoping to feel his heartbeat. "You need to feed."

"I am," Killian said. "I don't like the idea of leaving you alone."

"I won't be alone."

"Once all of this is over, let's go to the mountains," Killian suggested. "I have a cabin, and we can go away."

"Alright." she smiled.

"We are about to go feed." Isla knocked on the door. "Better go," Arabella said, keeping her eyes on Killian. "I love you." he bent down to kiss her lips. Her lips tasted like warm sugar.

He quickly pulls away and walks out of the room. Killian sees Julian standing in the foyer, hugging Isla and Caroline. How much he despised Julian, he knew that Julian was only protecting Arabella.

"Keep her safe," Killian said.

"I will," Julian said.

"If anything happens-

"Nothing will happen to her." Julian interrupted him. Killian looked back towards the stairs hoping to see Arabella before he left. She wasn't there. He sighed and walked towards the front door. Caroline and Isla were waiting inside the SUV. Walking towards it, he hears Arabella calling for him from behind.

"Wait," she yelled.

'What is it?" he asked, worried.

She ran towards him, almost knocking them both down, then said, "I want to be with you. I don't want anything else but you."

"I want to be with you too," Killian whispered.

"I love you, Killian," she says before forcefully kissing him.

As they both embrace the sweet moment, the time comes to a pause. Killian grips Arabella's waist tighter, pulling her closer to him. He doesn't want to let her go; she doesn't want him to.

They finally pull away, both grinning with joy. He kisses her one last time on the forehead and then whispers that he loves her in her ear. She smiled, her heart racing; it practically felt like it was going to burst out of her chest with excitement. She could never grow tired of hearing him say that he loved her. Arabella watched him get into the SUV and drive away. Why did she feel it was the last time she was going to see him? The thought made her feel uneasy. She walked inside and found Julian talking to Maisie.

"It took some convincing, but mom and dad are on board with you being here with Julian," Maisie informed her. "Noah and I have to go."

"Where are you staying?" Arabella asked.

"Noah's parents have a cabin by the lake. They agreed that we would be safe there." Maisie answered.

"How are they doing?" Arabella asked.

"They are still trying to get over the idea of their son not killing Julian and Killian when he had the chance, but his safety is what matters. Mine too." Maisie explained. "Let me know when you made it," Arabella told her.

"I will." Maisie hugged her sister tightly.

Julian and Arabella watched as Maisie and Noah left, leaving just them in the house. It was quiet; both didn't say a word. Arabella felt she owed Julian an apology, but she couldn't find the right words. After all, what were the right words? Arabella looked down at her phone; she had several missed calls from Eva. Eva, OMG! she thought. She forgot about the fundraiser. She forgot about Eva and Scott. Some best friend she was. Arabella had no choice but to keep Eva and Scott out of the loop; she was trying to protect them. But it seemed that the more she wanted to alleviate the situation, the people close to her ended up getting affected.

Arabella was in the bedroom, sitting on the window seat with the window open. She didn't mind the cool breeze hitting her face. She enjoyed it; the whistling noise the wind made, the sound of the leaves rustling. Arabella closed her eyes to breathe in the fresh air. It was the first time she felt at peace in months. Was that the wrong thing for her to say? Amid the chaos, she felt at ease. Was something terrible going to happen to her with her feeling like this? If that were the case, she would enjoy every minute of it. Arabella wasn't afraid of dying; she thought it was beautiful. She welcomed death. What terrified her the most was dying alone. She wanted to be surrounded by loved ones.

The unsettling thoughts of Tessa came flooding her mind. Tessa was going to make Arabella's death far from beautiful. Arabella managed to keep the thoughts at bay and focused on something else. Killian. His sweet voice brought butterflies to her stomach. Despite her having feelings for Julian, she is bound to Killian. She felt it when they kissed. And when he looked at her. Thoughts of the son she had flooded her mind. She wondered what he was like. She bet that he was the most beautiful in the world. Tears formed and rolled down her cheeks. She sat on the seat gazing out, letting the tears roll down her face.

"Hey," Julian said, knocking on the door softly.

Arabella quickly wiped her tears and looked up. "Thought you would have fallen asleep," he said. "Can't," she told him. She turned her head away to continue to look out the window.

"Everything will be alright." he sat in front of her. Without breaking her focus from the outside, she says, "How can you be so sure?"

"Trust me."

"Thank you." she looked at him. "For everything." she reached out to touch his hand. His body temperature didn't bother her anymore.

"It's getting late," he said, gently moving her hand to stand up. "Get some sleep."

He was right; it was after midnight. Somehow tonight didn't make Arabella tired. She nodded at him and then continued to look out the window.

"What do you see in him?" Julian asked.

"What?" Arabella said.

"You owe me why," he said.

"It's different with Killian."

"I just want you to be happy." he continued to walk out. Was Arabella happy, or was she hiding behind something? Or someone? Arabella sat at the window for another hour before climbing into bed. She lay there looking at the ceiling, the V-shaped grooves; she wondered how they were formed. Was she like the tracks? One minute she didn't know how she got here, but she was figuring it out. She was particular about one thing; her love for Killian. Destiny tied them together, and faith bound them. Killian made her feel extraordinary. He gave her excitement. The only response she could think would suffice to Julian's statement was that she was happy. She never felt better. She closes her eyes and goes to sleep.

Days have gone by, and no sign of Tessa. Arabella was starting to think something must've happened to her. Watching Killian climb into the SUV was her only memory of him. She could only pray that he was alright. She never talked about the pain she was feeling to Julian; she didn't want to upset him. But she knew he sensed her pain. He could feel it. Arabella has already felt like she hurt him enough by choosing Killian over him. Talking about her feelings to the man that loves her just the same as the man who never stopped loving her was bound to cause more damage. Every time Julian entered the room, Arabella quickly thought about something else. She was forced to think of something worth talking about. But Julian knew, and somehow, he understood it. And that's probably why her feelings for him evolved as they did because he didn't question or shout at her. Arabella and Julian both knew she had a spot for him. It just wasn't the same she had for Killian.

Arabella was sitting across from Julian at the kitchen table, reading her textbooks that her history teacher had assigned for reading. Her parents had told the school that there was a family emergency, so Maisie and I wouldn't be at school. Arabella glanced up and saw the November sun glisten on his skin. It was her first time seeing how beautiful he looked. He noticed that she was gawking at him. He didn't say a word. "The sun can't kill you," she said in amazement.

"No, not anymore."

"Why?"

"This." he rolled up his sleeve and showed her the tattoo; he then stood up, unbuttoning his shirt. He showed her another tattoo.

The tattoo looked familiar. Where did she see it? Killian has one on his back.

"What does it mean?" she asked, looking at the shapes and lines.

"The Cold Ones," he responded, "when we were created, a few vampires disobeyed the Order. They were sentenced to death. The ones that didn't were given a gift from a witch. She gave us the ability to walk in the sun without burning."

"Do you remember the day when you turned?"

"Yes," he replied. He buttoned his shirt and sat down. "What was it like?"

"Excruciating," he explained. "The woman who turned me-." he paused.

"Your lover?" Arabella asked.

"She wanted us to be together. She didn't want me to grow old; she said it would've killed her," he said. "She died helping vampires flee from the hunters."

"I'm sorry, Julian," she said. "What was her name?" "Clarisa." he stood up, grabbed his textbook, and started walking but stopped and turned to look at Arabella. "You think I wouldn't pick up the hints?" "Julian, you don't understand." she stood up.

"It's suicide," he exclaimed. "Have you told Killian?" "He doesn't know," she answered. "And you aren't going to tell him."

"Why do you want to? You'll have to feed on human blood, that is, if you can't control it."

"You don't think I can do it?" she asked angrily.

"A vampire bite is different from anything else. It's like being chosen. If it doesn't accept you, then it will kill you." he informed her. "You can't just want it; it has to want you." he turned around and headed out of the room.

Arabella hadn't thought about it thoroughly. She just knew she wanted to become what they were. And what did Julian know? Nothing. She stormed upstairs and slammed the bedroom door behind her. She paced around the room, contemplating her decision. She knew she craved it more than anything. Why was Julian giving her a hard time?

Suddenly Arabella's phone rings. Without reading the caller ID, she answers it.

"Hello," Arabella said.

"Bella," Eva said breathlessly.

Eva was at home; she hadn't heard from Arabella in several days and was starting to get worried. The last thing she told Arabella was that she was always trying to gain attention. Why would she say that? Was it because if something went right, Arabella turned it on herself? They had been friends for years, and Eva couldn't imagine not talking to her. Eva was never jealous of Arabella. But the one time Eva felt things were finally going her way, her friend wasn't there to support her.

Eva had invited Scott over; she knew he would keep her from getting down.

Eva walked into the kitchen to cook the popcorn. She heard the doorbell ring; she looked down at her phone. Scott was early.

"It's open," Eva shouted from the kitchen.

Tessa opened the door and walked in. She could smell salty popcorn cooking from the kitchen. She followed the stench and saw Eva; her back was to her.

"You're early," Eva said.

Tessa watched as Eva poured the popcorn into a white bowl. She turned around and gasped when she saw Tessa standing there so lifelike.

"Hey, Eva." Tessa smiled. She whacked Eva in the face and watched her body hit the kitchen floor.

Scott had brought flowers to his date. As he walked towards Eva's front door, he smoothed his shirt. He reached the door; the door was slightly opened. He pushes it, letting himself in.

"Eva," he shouts.

No one answered. Scott shouted her name again; no answer. He walked into the kitchen; he noticed that there was popcorn on the floor. Scott walks towards it and immediately sees Eva lying on the floor unconscious. He rushes to her.

"Oh, Scott," Tessa said behind him.

Scott turned around, and Tessa slammed his head against the cabinet.

Tessa takes Eva and Scott to where the accident occurred. She bonds their hands together, reaches into Eva's pockets, and takes her phone out. She dials Arabella's number and waits for her to pick it up. "Hello, " Arabella says.

Tessa put the phone to Eva's ear and jerked her around so she would speak.

"Bella," Eva said.

"Eva, is everything alright?" Arabella asked. "Everything is not alright," Tessa answered. "Eva and her beloved Scott are tied up at the moment."

"Tessa, what do you want?" Arabella asked.

"I want you to give me my life back," Tessa screamed into the phone.

"I can't. I wish I could."

"Since you can't, I'm going to take one from you," Tessa explained. "Who's it going to be? Eva or Scott?"

"No," Arabella shouted. "I can meet you anywhere. Just name a place."

"Where it all happened," Tessa said.

Arabella quickly ran downstairs.

"What's the rush?" Julian asked.

"It's Tessa. She has Eva and Scott," she told him.

"I'm going with you." he grabbed his keys.

She didn't want to argue with him. They both ran out of the house and got into the truck.

Arabella took out her phone and dialed Killian's number. He didn't pick up, but she waited until the female voice recorder told her to stay after the beep to leave a voicemail.

"Hey, it's me," she said. "I'm about to do something foolish. I love you, Killian." she hurried and ended the message. She tucked her phone in her pocket. She glanced at Julian and said, "If anything happens to me, tell Killian I love him."

"He wouldn't let me live if anything happened to you," Julian told her.

Arabella smiled because she knew that was true. Killian would do anything to protect her.

Julian slowed the truck to a stop. He parked several feet from the bridge. He turned to look at Arabella, who was already looking at him.

"Noah and Maisie are on their way," Julian told her. Arabella nodded, and Julian watched her get out of the truck and start walking towards the bridge.

"Glad you make it," Tessa said.

"Bella!" Eva screamed.

"It's alright," Arabella said.

"Is it, Bella?" Tessa asked. "You have changed since the last time I saw you. You have a vampire as a lover."

"I can say the same about you," Arabella said. "What happened to you?"

"Wouldn't you like to know?" Tessa said. "He saved my life. I am forever in his debt."

"Who?" Arabella asked, walking closer to her. "Who turned you?"

"This isn't about me. You stopped making it about me when you didn't show up to my funeral. I thought we were best friends."

"We are."

"No, Bell. We were. You thought I was dead. You left me to die. You all did." Tessa corrected. "I gave my last breath when they put me in the body bag."

"What do you want me to say?" Arabella cried.

"I want you and your vampire. You thought I couldn't smell him?" Tessa asked. "Come out."

A minute later, Julian appeared from behind the woods. He walked towards Arabella keeping his eyes on Tessa.

"You're not him," Tessa said, disappointed. She walked towards Eva and Scott, holding her claws on Eva's neck.

"No," Arabella screamed.

"You need to choose," Tessa yelled.

"I can't." Arabella softly cried.

"I'll choose for you," Tessa said. A silver arrow struck her chest as she was about to rip Eva's throat. She quickly stumbled backward, trying to take the arrow out.

"Get Eva and Scott," Julian demanded.

Arabella ran towards Eva, unbound her hands, and did the same for Scott. Arabella looked behind and saw Noah walking towards them, holding a bow. Maisie was walking with him.

"What is going on?" Eva asked.

"Vampire Hunter," Tessa said. "I didn't see that one coming." she ran towards Noah, trying to take him out. But Julian stood in her way, causing her to miss and hit the pavement hard.

Julian pulled Tessa to her feet, almost tearing her blouse. Tessa raised her arms, grabbed Julian, and swung him over her, slamming him on his back. Noah threw his right fist at Tessa's temple. He realized it only made her angrier. Tessa put her hand around Noah's throat, raising him off the ground and forcing the oxygen to stop flowing. Julian stood up and tackled Tessa.

"Noah," Maisie yelled.

"No." Arabella held her back.

Arabella noticed the wooden stake Noah had fallen out of his back pocket. She quickly ran to it and yelled his name. Noah saw that Arabella had the stake and would toss it to him. She threw it, and he caught it. Tessa had thrown Julian down and started walking towards Arabella.

"Enough," she shouted. "You are the only person I needed."

As she started running towards Arabella, Noah ran after her. Tessa swung, and Arabella landed several feet away. Noah jumped and aimed the stake toward Tessa's heart. The stake went through, forcing Tessa to collapse onto the pavement. Noah quickly ran to Maisie and hugged her. Suddenly they all heard tires screeching. A black Lexus had stopped quickly, and Killian got out. Caroline got out and was followed by Isla. The three of them ran to Julian.

"Where is she?" Killian yelled.

Julian didn't say anything. Killian asked again. "Killian," Arabella said, stumbling towards him. "Arabella." Killian let go of Julian and ran to her. He noticed that she was severely bruised.

Arabella and Killian walked toward Tessa's body. "What do we do now?" Noah asked.

"Burn the body," Isla answered.

An hour later, they brought Tessa's corpse to the field. They had several logs of wood by her body. Arabella watched as Julian and Noah lit the wood, and the flame traveled onto the body. Arabella watched as Eva dropped her head on Scott's shoulder. Noah wrapped his arm around Maisie. Caroline and Isla were making sure the body burned thoroughly. Killian held out his hand for Arabella to take; she did and smiled.

They were all sitting in Julian's kitchen in silence an hour later. Neither one spoke. What could they say? What was the right thing to say in a time like this? Arabella couldn't help but feel like she had let everyone down. She put them in danger.

"So you're a vampire?" Eva asked Julian breaking the silence.

"Yeah," he answered.

"I'm sorry for not telling you," Arabella said. "I was trying to protect you both."

"I forgive you," Scott said. "It was creepy seeing Tessa." "Do you know who turned her?" Eva asked.

"We were trying to figure that out," Caroline said. "What are we going to do for Thanksgiving?" Scott asked.

Arabella could see Killian standing on the front porch from the kitchen window. She excused herself from the Thanksgiving conversation and walked outside.

"Hey, " she said. She placed her hand on his back. "How are you?" he asked, looking down at her. He gently rubbed her bruised face. "What were you thinking? You could've been killed."

"Killian, I'm okay," she assured him. "Better now that you are here."

Killian pulled her closer to him and kissed her head. "Some birthday," she said. She pulled away and then looked up at him. "Killian, I want you to turn me."

His eyes grew wide. For the longest, he didn't say anything. He pulled her to him, and they stared into the distance listening to the wind blow. Arabella was unsure whether or not Killian understood what she asked him, but she knew that was a conversation for another day.

The thought that did seem to make its way to Arabella's mind countless times today was that Tessa knew who Killian was. Arabella wanted to know why she wanted Killian. Arabella stood there wrapped in Killian's arms, thinking about Tessa. She couldn't help but feel that Killian was hiding something from her. But the answers she yearned for weren't going to come from him.

It was winter break in Evergreen Springs, and Arabella couldn't have been more than relieved. As she walked through the high school halls, she could see the students saying their goodbyes to one another. Some even asked each other what their plans were for the two weeks. What were Arabella's plans? Maybe she was going to confine herself to the four walls she called her bedroom. Or perhaps she would tag along with Maisie and Noah; she heard they were going camping. Whatever Arabella's plans were, she couldn't possibly think about leaving Killian's side. There were nights when Arabella would wake in a sweat because of a nightmare about Killian. Some were Killian dying, and the others were disappearing, leaving her to face the troubles alone. But when she would wake, he was there, there holding her. He comforted her, gently rubbing her head. And even with that, she still felt miles away from him.

Arabella saw Eva and Scott leaning against his pickup truck.

"Hey," Eva said. "What are your plans for the break?" "Going to Syracuse." Arabella lied. She wasn't traveling anywhere; she was going to stay in Toronto. How much she wanted to travel miles away from the town, she couldn't leave.

"It'll be nice to get away from this town," Scott told her. "Where are you two headed?" Arabella asked.

"Going to Seattle." Eva looked at Scott and smiled.

"My uncle has a lake house, so we thought it would be good if we went with my family," Scott explained. "We better get going. Don't want to have them waiting."

"I'll see you both after the break," Arabella said. She hugged both of them, watched as they got into the truck, and drove out of the parking lot.

Twenty minutes later, Arabella was sitting in her room getting her head started on her homework when her dad knocked on her door.

"Hey, Bell," he said. "Do you plan on staying in for the two weeks?"

"I don't know. That seems to be like a good idea at the moment," she answered.

"Did something happened...between you and Killian?" he asked hesitantly.

Arabella smiled and said, "No, everything is OK. It has just been a hectic few months."

"If it helps any, your mother and I are proud of you and your sister."

"Thanks, dad."

"Go outside and live a little," he said, rolling his eyes. "Or whatever you kids' are doing."

"I'll keep that in mind."

Arabella watched as he walked out of her room, and when he heard his footsteps on the stairs, she continued to do her homework. But Arabella's mind wasn't focused. Seriously, what was she doing? She threw her homework off to the side of her and let out a sigh. She wanted to go out and have fun. She wanted to be those girls that let their hair down. Arabella deserved it; she deserved to be happy. But in all honesty, she just wanted to be with Killian. Everyone was off doing something, and she was thinking about Killian; Maisie was with Noah, Eva and Scott left for Seattle, and Julian, well, Arabella, didn't know what he was doing. The last she spoke to him was Thanksgiving. He had told her that he and his family were leaving to discuss their stay in Toronto with The Council. Arabella looked through her phone; there were several text messages from her to Julian. He didn't answer a single one. Arabella didn't blame him. How could she? Arabella knew he must hate her for causing him to feel like he had a chance. Tears began to roll down her cheeks. She just needed to see if he was okay. Images of Julian flooded her head. She realized it was the only thing she had of him. Why was she feeling like this? She may love Killian, but she also has a love for Julian.

Abruptly, Arabella's phone rings. She snapped back into reality and looked down at the caller ID; Killian, it read. She slid the phone key to the right and placed the phone to her ear.

"I was just thinking about you," she said.

"Good things, I hope," he said back.

Arabella could hear the happiness in his voice.

"Where are you?" she asked. "I want to see you." "Come outside," he told her.

Arabella grabbed her coat and went downstairs. Her parents were in the kitchen reading the afternoon paper. Arabella opened the front door with her phone attached to her ear. Killian was standing outside, leaning against his car. He wore a black suede coat complemented by a black sweatshirt and faded jeans. There was something different about him.

"What are you going here?" she shouted from the porch.

"I believe we had a deal. You were supposed to come away with me," he responded.

"I have to pack. I would need clothes." she walked down the porch steps making her way to him.

"Good thing, it is already done for you." he smiled. His eyes shifted behind her.

Arabella followed his eyes and saw her parents standing in the doorway. They were both smiling at her.

"You did this?" she asked them.

"We may have our differences, but one thing we can agree on is that we want you to be happy," Tom said. Arabella ran to her parents and hugged them both before running toward Killian.

"Where are we going?" she asked Killian.

"It's a surprise," he answered. He opened her door for her, and Arabella got in.

Several hours later, Killian drove on to a landing area. There were several helicopters lined in front of the bay. Killian kept driving until a helicopter with a man was next to it. He put the car in park and got out. Arabella watched him walk to her door and open it.

"What are we doing here?" she asked nervously.

"Monsieur Winter." the gentleman from the helicopter said. "The chopper is fueled and ready to go."

"Thank you, Antoine," Killian said.

Arabella noticed that Antoine had the same tattoo as Killian peeking out from his unbuttoned collar shirt. Antoine caught her staring, and Arabella quickly looked away. Killian gestured for her to wait in the helicopter, and she did. She fastened the belt around her waist and across her chest, then gazed out the window. Killian was speaking to Antoine; then he hugged Antoine. Arabella watched as Killian grabbed their duffel bags, walked to the helicopter, and placed them inside. A minute later, Killian opened the cockpit door and climbed inside. Arabella watched as Killian flicked on the switches, then the sound of the propellers filled the air.

"Salinas Tower, this is Winters W44 helicopter EC120 ready for departure?" Killian said into the headset.

"Winters W44, this is Salinas Tower. You are set for takeoff." the male voice said on the other end of the radio.

Killian raised the lever upward, and Arabella felt a tug at the belt strap, then the helicopter quickly lifted from the ground.

Once the helicopter was in the air, Arabella gazed out the window in amazement. The sun was setting, which made for a beautiful view. The ground was visible to Arabella; she could see a panoramic view of the valleys and mountains. She was uncomfortably cramped in the seat, but that somehow went away as she continued to look at the view they were flying over. The humming noise from the propellers was soothing to her. It was her helicopter ride, and she wanted to savor every minute of it. As the sun plunged underneath the skyline, the momentary shades of nightfall started to disappear. Arabella could see in the distance the sloping of the mountains. The sun was a crisp circle giving off a blue pigment on the hills.

Hours later, Killian gently held the throttle downward, and the helicopter descended onto the pavement. A red-haired gentleman greeted them once Killian turned off the propellers and shut down the panels. "Mr. Winters." the gentleman said.

"Lachlan, this is Arabella Holloway. She will be accompanying me to the cabin. Make her feel welcome." Killian told him.

"Of course, Sir." Lachlan looked at Arabella and smiled. He had the same tattoo on his neck.

Lachlan escorted them to a black Audi parked feet away from the helicopter. Killian opened the passenger door, and Arabella got in. She had many questions about Antoine and Lachlan. She wondered if they were more of them. Of course, they were, she thought.

Killian was driving along a rocky pavement. Arabella could hear the sound of the snow crunching against the tires. Killian drove for fifteen minutes before reaching a two-story cabin. Killian stopped the car in front of the front doors. He walked towards the passenger door, opened it, and Arabella was in awe of the cabin. The scenery was beautiful and quiet. Through the stained-glass windows, Arabella could see a decorated Christmas tree. She could smell the freshness of the crisp air as if she could almost taste it.

"Go inside," Killian told her. "I'll get the bags." Arabella smiled and walked to the double doors. She opened them, pushed them inward, and walked in. Arabella walked into a clean room with polished wood cupboards and counters. The sink in the kitchen was stainless steel. The antler lights reflected off the polished floor in each room. The furniture was antique but quaint. Arabella walked out to the patio. There was a clear view of the mountains and the water. She noticed a deer had peeked from behind the tree and realized that

Killian hadn't fed. She turned around and stopped when she saw Killian standing there. She noticed how black his eyes were.

"You need to feed." She demanded.

"I will." He said softly.

She walked towards him.

"I don't want you to see me like this." He turned his head away from her.

"You don't frighten me."

"I'll be back in twenty minutes," he told her. "Go inside." he gently led her inside, and when she turned around, he was gone.

Later that night, Arabella showered; she was exhausted from the helicopter ride; she wanted to sleep, but she wanted to wait for Killian. She walked into the kitchen; she was famished. She opened the stainless-steel refrigerator; there was enough food in there to feed an army. Why did Killian need so much food? She asked herself. Arabella walked over to the phone plugged in on the counter; she looked down at the number list on a piece of journal paper. Arabella pressed one dial and waited.

"Hello?" a man said.

"Hi, I'm staying in the cabin, " Arabella begins to say, "can I have a cheese pizza delivered?"

"Right away, Miss Holloway." the man said. "Anything else?"

"No," she answered.

The man then ends the call.

As Arabella examined the house, she noticed an antique trunk next to one cupboard. She walked towards it and opened it. There were senior portraits and discarded letters inside. She held up one of the photographs; it was a picture of her, Killian, and their son.

"He was beautiful," Killian said behind him.

Arabella jumped and turned her head to look at him. "What is all this?"

"Letters I wrote to you but never sent. I had given you a camera, and you told me you wanted to savor every moment." Killian knelt beside her.

"What was he like?" Arabella looked down at the portrait of Archie.

"A lot like you," he responded. "He was independent. The only person he wanted to be next to was you." "Killian," she said.

"You don't have to tell me. I already know," he told her. He stood up and walked towards the kitchen.

"You can't change my mind," she told him. She followed him into the kitchen.

"I wasn't going to. I know you want me to turn you." "Are you?"

"Food is here," he said, raising his head. He could hear the sound of tires screeching.

Killian opened the door to greet the dark-haired man. Killian reached into his pocket, gave the man a tip, and then closed the door. Killian placed the pizza box on the counter, took a slice out, and placed it on a plate before handing it to Arabella. Arabella took a bite of the pizza; she was so hungry.

"I'll turn you," he told her.

"You will?" she asked.

"But it'll be on my terms," he added.

"Deal," she said. "Can I ask you something?"

Killian raised his eyebrows, waiting for her to ask the question.

"Antoine and Lachlan have the same tattoos as you and Julian. Does that mean there are more of you?"

"Yes, just a few," he answered.

"Antoine didn't seem to be impressed when he saw me."

"He's protective. He doesn't want you to discuss our identity with anyone." Killian explained. "We have lived in the shadows for centuries, made a living among the humans."

"I can see that." Arabella looked around the cabin. "The second time I found you, we discussed running away with Archie. You said you wanted to live in a cabin with the finest clothes and furniture. Archie was supposed to have his room surrounded by the most delicate musical instruments." Killian said. "When you left, and Archie died, I built this house. I figured that when I finish, you will come back. I will hear a knock at the door, and I will open it, and you would be standing there with Archie."

Arabella didn't say a word.

"You must be tired," he said. "Come on." he took her hand and led her upstairs to a bedroom. "This is where you'll sleep."

"You're not sleeping here?" she asked.

"I'll be next door," he responded. "I promised your parents that I would bring you back in one piece. Goodnight."

"Goodnight."

Later that night, Arabella lay awake staring at the ceiling. She reached for her phone; it was 11:30 pm.

Even though she was tired, she couldn't go to sleep. She thought about Archie. How happiest he must've been and how helpless he was when he died. She begins to cry. Suddenly, there is a knock on the door. "Arabella," Killian said.

"I'm fine," she said. "Please go."

She was tired of things being taken away from her. She didn't know how long she had with Killian before he was taken away from her too. Arabella didn't know exactly when, but she felt it coming. She prayed that she would be able to prevent it. All she wanted to do was live forever with him.

The End

OTHER BOOKS BY THE AUTHOR

Karmic Love

Undercover

Eternal Love

Undying Lust

The Good Taste

Offence and Justice

A Model for Murder

Lethal Legacy

Lethal Legacy 2

Paranormal Club

Enchanted Souls

Beginners of Nowhere

Wildflower

Mystic Agent

Dark Angel

Lonesome Moonlight

The Eerie Egg

A Romantic Crime

Passionate Alien

The Critical Case